Lark's Castle

Also by Susannah York

IN SEARCH OF UNICORNS

LARK'S CASTLE

by

SUSANNAH YORK

Illustrations by Michael Baldwin

David McKay Company, Inc.

New York

Library of Congress Catalog Card Number: 76–25761
ISBN: 0–679–20383–4

Printed in Great Britain

For

SASHA

with love

1

The shutters were closed like all the shutters now, but Lark could see Sarah through the slats. The little girl stood outside on the grass, staring back so sadly at the moonlit château that Lark longed to leap down from the kitchen range and run out to her in the park. 'Never mind, never mind,' she'd cry, 'we'll come back.'

If only she'd been born a person! Since the day she'd been carved, Lark had had these impossible longings. The questions she could never ask at school (Sarah took her every day in her satchel), the ideas she'd suddenly long to shout out, the awfulness of not holding a pencil yourself, turning the pages of a book, running races, playing tag, climbing trees! All she was learning and couldn't share — yes, that was the worst, not *sharing* it with the bear and the rabbit, and the rest of the toys in the Battersea cupboard which was home. And *that's*, the wooden doll thought for the thousandth time, that's what it was being a toy. You saw things, you felt things, you wanted and heard and thought things, but you could never, ever tell them or do anything about them at all.

But really it wasn't sadness she was feeling, propped up there against the fluepipe on the range: excitement burst over her in little bubbles. Home, she was going home! Lovely, lovely holidays, but now she was going home.

All about she could hear the noises of the family leaving; Tom dragging his bag down the passage and slopping the water from his tadpole-jar, Mrs Stern running upstairs, downstairs, outside and back again, she could hear the car starting up, and a valley away she heard the village clock strike midnight.

Pop! Mr Stern switched off the electricity at the mains, everything went dark. The little château ('a toy château' the house-agent had said and Sarah called it 'Lark's Castle') seemed to be sighing farewell from deep under its layers of peeling paint and now, *now*, thought the little wooden doll, in Sarah would dash, scoop her up, and off they would drive in the night, Dieppe, the English Channel and London.

'Goodbye, lovely place,' whispered the little girl out in the park, 'lovely, *lovely* place!' Then she gave a sudden ear-splitting shriek.

8

'Oh look, look everybody — look, there's a witch flying over the chimney and she's flying on a snow-white goose!' She rushed over to her mother who was rummaging in the car, and dragged her back across the grass. 'Look, look, her cloak's blowing out in the moonlight!'

'How wonderful.' Juliet Stern was a young sort of mother. 'I haven't seen a witch for years.' Indeed, a big white thing *was* flapping over the roof. A goose, a farmyard goose? It must be an owl. And — yes, it really did look very much as though something were on it, as though a huge black bat were astride the goose! The owl. A bat on an owl, a witch on a goose...

Tom who didn't believe in witches or not that they flew, had come scrambling out of the car.

'Golly, *golly,* I do believe Sarah's right! It *is* a witch,' he whistled.

'She's circling, she's going to land on the turret!' Up and down Sarah hopped, but just then a vast black cloud sailed across the moon and Lark, who was peering through the shutters as hard as she could, could see nothing, and outside the children and their mother could see nothing, and Mr Stern who'd been fiddling with the engine, looked in the car and saw no one was there. He let out a bellow.

'Juliet, Tom, Sarah, for heaven's sake hurry up, we've got to get going!'

'But Daddy, there's a witch on the chimney, and she's flying on a —'

'I don't care if there's a dragon in the wainscot, we've got to catch that morning boat. Juliet, get the children in the car.'

9

'Oh goodness, *Lark,* I nearly forgot Lark!' And Sarah went rushing back into the château where just at that moment an extraordinary thing was happening.

An icy wind had come howling down the chimney, causing Lark to rock back and forth, back and forth against the fluepipe on the range until with the force of a gale it knocked her down. She rolled over the edge and fell straight into a pile of soot in the old fireplace behind; then a cackle like the cry of a banshee came spiralling down the chimney, and Sarah burst into the kitchen.

The little girl stopped at once for she could see nothing, but as if at some signal, a piece of plaster fell straight out of the ceiling and hit her on the temple, making her stagger and clutch the door: she began to shiver violently. The kitchen that for a whole month had been full of daytime sunlight, smells of bread and casseroles and fresh French coffee, had become in minutes a cold, unfriendly place. And utterly black. Not a slither of moonlight came through the shutters, while all about her hung echoes of secret laughter like the last dings of a fearful bell.

Trembling, she felt her way over to the range. It was silly to be afraid of the dark, and she was sure Lark was there.

'Daddy,' she cried as her father swooped into the kitchen with his torch, 'I can't find Lark!'

'Your mother must have packed her.' He picked up the struggling Sarah as though she were a feather.

'But I put her here, I know I did, I leaned her up against the fluepipe — Daddy please, *please,* I can't go without Lark!'

10

'Here, here,' everything in Lark was shouting out, 'I'm here in the fireplace.' But neither Sarah nor her father could hear and Mr Stern said, 'Then your mother or Tom has picked her up. Come on, Sarah, it's long after midnight!' Out of the kitchen he strode with her, slamming the back door with such force that the château seemed to shake in its foundations.

'Daddy!' Lark heard the little girl wail, and, the anxious voice of Juliet Stern drifted through the shutters, 'Oh I'm sure we've forgotten something.'

'Me, me, you've forgotten *me!*' the soul of the wooden doll cried out, but no sound came from her mouth and with a roar the car leapt away down the grassy drive, into the night.

To feel a thousand tears inside and not be able to cry them, is a very bad feeling indeed, but if you're a human being there are things you can do instead. You can whistle, dance a jig, fly a kite, dig a flowerbed, and as long as you do it hard enough people will ask you why, and thinking up reasons, you won't think of your tears. Then one fine day you'll discover they've escaped without your noticing and there are no more left inside.

But Lark couldn't do any of those things and she felt her heart would burst. Never to go to school again in Sarah's satchel! Be stuffed in a pocket climbing trees, never see the toys, or the Battersea ducks, ride in a bus, share Sarah's adventures and lessons, secrets and tears. Sarah had gone.

Everything was very black indeed.

'Hee, hee, that'll fix 'em, Skite!'

Ermyntrude, last witch of Rezay (that part of France where Lark's Castle stood) sat on the chimney-pot snickering, which was unwise for she was extremely fat, and the chimney-pot like everything else about the château needed repair. Her plump horny legs swung to and fro in time with the snickers.

'Nasty, horrid family. Nasty, horrid little girl. Horrid, *horrid* wooden doll!' Skite, the goose she'd stolen from a farmer's wife a couple of hundred years ago rubbed his back against the turret, and pretended to understand nothing of his mistress's glee; Skite was good at minding his own business. Anyway, his back ached.

'"Lark's Castle"' indeed,' Ermyntrude snorted. 'It's *my* castle, Ermyntrude's castle, it's been mine for years and years. Nasty old Vicomte letting it out, nasty, nasty house-agent. Well, ho, ho, Lark's in her castle and she'll never get out again — "Lark's Castle", my *broomstick!*'

'You haven't got one,' Skite reminded her painfully, twisting his beak to massage his back; Ermyntrude really ought to go on a diet.

'Don't answer back.' But she was in too good a mood to whack him, and instead she climbed to her enormous

feet and began a slow, old-fashioned, very unsafe-looking jig along the chimney-pots.

Black, blacker, blackest of blacks. Certainly the soot was, Lark was half-buried in it and she couldn't see much of the ceiling, only the rafters, and they were covered in cobwebs. Spiders too, probably, and though she wasn't particularly fond of spiders, she thought she'd be quite glad to see one — anything to take her mind off this loneliness, and the terrible armies of tears gathering and gathering inside. A mouse, Mr Stern was always grumbling about the mice, please let there be a mouse.

And most obligingly at that very moment came a scuttle.

But it didn't come from her level, it came from somewhere high up, a long way above her head. In fact it seemed to be coming from the chimney.

Scuttle, scuttle, rattle...here it came, help, it was *racing!* Bang, rattle, it must be a terribly long chimney, scuttle, bang, whistle, oh help, ping, skid, ow, it was going to spring on her, leap at her, ouch she was stuck, there was nothing she could do — suddenly whatever it was, stopped. There was a sort of light, groaning sound as though something were rolling itself off a ledge, then rattle, whistle, plop! The thing had fallen into her lap.

It was hard, that was certain, very small and hard — was it simply a stone?

And while she lay there helpless in the soot, a dazzling blue light shattered the darkness and went on shattering it, as though a thousand splinters of glass were being flung over and over again against every

13

surface and cranny of the gloomy kitchen, and at the same time Lark felt an extraordinary tingling sensation in her feet. It began very faintly, and it was as if (she thought afterwards) hundreds of ants were uncurling themselves in her toes, uncurling and stretching and beginning to wander: along her feet, round and round her ankles, up her shins and knees, and all the way along her legs and body...

Up through her chest they milled and marched on tiny hurrying feet, dividing at her throat and some turning left and some to right, down to the tips of her fingers; then back, back and up through the little wooden neck — cheeks, nostrils, forehead, eyes, the little dome at the back of her head, until every bit of her, every single particle of wood in her felt wondrously, shoutingly, incredulously alive!

A ribbon of coolness came slipping down her throat, already she was breathing in faint tiny pants, and all this while the blue smithereens of light shattered on and on around her, and from very far away, a long way up the top of the chimney the most dreadful sounds cascaded down, echoing and re-echoing through the kitchen.

'Pockets with holes, a plague on them all, cursed be all jigs on a chimney! Lost it, lost it, the stone of Life — ah, Lifestone, my Lifestone!' On and on shrieked the voice, and if Lark had not been so excited she'd have been terribly afraid, but her hand shot out into the blue glancing light, and as suddenly down again into the powdery stuff she was lying on, and she could feel it, she could *feel* the soot soft and damp in her fingers, and she heard a voice shout out 'I can feel it, oh I can, I

14

can!', a new voice clear as bells; with a shudder of delight she realised it was her own.

The shock had jerked her up, and now she saw in the faded cotton folds of her smock what was causing these astonishing things to happen. A tiny stone lay glittering there, brighter than the sapphire on Mrs Stern's ring, bluer than any sky or eye she'd ever seen.

And even as she sat there staring, the fragments of light that had splintered all about her sprang back, as though drawn to the stone by an invisible force. Like an exploding star the Lifestone paled; paler and paler it grew until it seemed no more than a rather pretty cloudy pebble, such as you might find on any beach.

2

Out slipped the moon from under a cloud like a tennis ball: Ermyntrude had turned green as a jelly.

'Frogspawn and vipers' tongues,' she cried in a trembling croak, 'I'll have to go down the chimney after it.' It would be a frightful squeeze and she was terrified, but there was no help for it. She had stolen the Lifestone from a tremendously powerful wizard thousands of moons ago, and she knew that if a second dew were to dry on the grass before she held it again, its powers for her must fade. For when the Lifestone acknowledged a new master its former owner must become mortal again — subject to time, disease, accident, death.

'Avaunt, ye last witch of Rezay!' she cried, but just then Skite, who was a highly-strung sort of goose, had a fit of hysterics. The high-pitched chortles rang out across the park, and the sight of the giggling, gleaming beak was too much for the old witch: with a shriek she fell off the chimney and bounced down to the gutter. And if Skite had been a goose without a conscience, the story of Lark's Castle would have been very different.

But he wasn't.

As Ermyntrude clung to the gutter, he cruised down to hover just below her. She let go with a groan (she'd been about to anyway), and they returned to the chimney.

'Numbskull! Skeleton! I'll teach you to smirk. Aye, aye, snigger away, snigger at my misfortune. Who was it gave you life, you flea-ridden excuse for a broom-stick?' she gasped. 'To whom do you owe your two hundred years and more? To me, me, Ermyntrude, Keeper of the Lifestone, last witch of Rezay. You fishbone, you toastrack, you need the Lifestone as much as I!'

And Skite did need the Lifestone, he wanted *life*, even if life meant Ermyntrude; peasant and prince, goose and gosling he had seen snatched away by time and the thought of that huge dark door into the Great Beyond frightened him horribly, for he wasn't even sure there was a Beyond. He tucked his beak in his chest, humiliated, but Ermyntrude's attention had returned to the chimney.

'Lifestone, little Lifestone, where are you, little treasure? Chirrup, chirrup, chirrup, tweet, tweet, tweet, shine for Ermyntrude — bounce up to Ermyntrude.'

17

But the Lifestone lay, dim and still in the listening doll's lap. Stealthily, unsteadily, Lark clambered to her feet, and oh the wonder of being able to move! Then as she stood trembling with excitement in the dark kitchen she heard sounds of grunting and heaving and squeezing, just as if the owner of the terrible voice were trying to get down the chimney.

She was, but she'd got stuck; Skite pulled her out.

'Now look here, Ermyntrude, you know perfectly well you can't get down that chimney, you haven't for years,' Skite said. 'And while we're on the subject, you ought to go on a diet.'

'Shan't,' snapped Ermyntrude. 'All right, you bag of bones, you go!'

Skite wished he'd kept his beak shut; he peered nervously down the chimney but he was too proud to refuse, and besides as Ermyntrude had pointed out, he needed the Lifestone too.

He shut his eyes and took a nosedive...

...plunged through a crow's nest, what was almost a safety-net of cobwebs, dislodged a bunch of bats (Skite was terrified of bats, there was something a deal too magical about mice who could fly), bruised his wing, twisted his ankle, chipped his beak and landed in the fireplace a choking, spluttering bundle of feathers, cobwebs, and soot.

'A wreck, that's what I am, a nervous wreck!' He got to his feet, soothed and dusted himself, and peered cautiously about. Moonlight was streaming in through the shutters now and in the middle of a flagstone stood Lark, looking startled but relieved.

'Hrrrrmph!' It bothered him to arrive so ruffled,

and anyway he hurt. 'I'm quite all right, thank you.'

'I *am* glad. It sounded very sore,' said Lark. 'I thought you might be the witch.'

'My mistress, Ermyntrude, she couldn't make it. And as a matter of fact, it was. I'm Skite.'

'And I'm Lark. So are you, er — er, are you her servant?' A witch's goose, was it dangerous?

'Confidant and friend,' Skite wasn't going to tell this inquisitive doll he might as well be a broomstick for all the notice Ermyntrude took of him. 'I ferry her about, and mind your own business.'

'I certainly will,' said Lark, though she thought him rather rude. 'I just don't happen to know any geese or witches, and you've got a cobweb hanging over your left eye.'

'Now look here —'

'Keep still. There. Oh dear,' Lark said, 'you are a mess, shall I clean you up? Would you like me to rub anything?'

'Now, look *here* —' but at that moment a bellow came down the chimney.

'Skite, you whey-faced chicken's picking, get up here with my Lifestone!'

'Oh, what a horrible voice, she's not very polite. And speaking of voices —' yes, speaking of voices, what was a doll doing *talking*? Before Skite could work it out, Ermyntrude bellowed down again.

'At the double, Skite, or I'll skin you alive.'

'At once. Immediately. Oh dear, oh dear, she'll dance all over my poor webbed feet. It all comes of doing a jig on a chimney-pot and not mending holes in your pocket.'

'Doing a *jig* — ?'

'Yes, you see she'd *got* you, she was gloating, the plan had worked — that's, er, that's to say, oo-er.' The goose had gone very red. He said hurriedly, 'I'm looking for a stone, quite small, very ordinary. No importance at all. Just that it fell down the chimney and might have rolled your way.'

So it was Ermyntrude who had caused Sarah to abandon her. There'd been magic afoot, it wasn't an accident but part of some grand design!

'I'll help you look.' Lark closed her fingers tightly round the Lifestone, she wasn't going to give it up now, and while Skite delved around in the grate she walked up and down through clouds of soot, peering along cracks in the flagstone.

'Skite, you scrawny cat's leavings, what are you doing down there?' screeched Ermyntrude. 'You're plotting, I know you're plotting. Bring me my Lifestone immediately.'

'Oh, oh, oh.' Round and round the kitchen the goose began to flap and squawk. 'I can't go back up that chimney, oh my nerves, oh that chimney, oh I'm a wreck, nobody knows what I suffer — and oh I can't go back without the Lifestone, she'll kill me if I don't find it!'

'She can't kill you, she needs you, you're her confidant and friend! You ferry her about, she *needs* you!' Round and round after the goose Lark ran, — and it was true, long ago Ermyntrude had lost the knack of riding a broomstick, but Skite was not to be comforted.

'No, no, no, I must find that stone. Oh that chimney'll be the death of me. Lifestone, Lifestone, for moon's sake, shine! Oh, if only there were another way out.'

'There is.'

'Don't be silly.' Skite skidded to a halt and rounded on Lark. 'If there was another way in or out of this château, you can bet your last tail-feather Ermyntrude would have found it; she's been trying to get in for years.'

'But why, what's so important in the château?'

What indeed. Skite gave an angry smirk. He knew what, all right. Ermyntrude wanted to visit all the wretched toys she'd locked in the attic of Lark's Castle, she wanted to scratch them and pinch them, twist their arms and gloat, knowing they couldn't fight back: she wanted to trample and dance on them just as she had when she'd been young and slim and powerful, and able to get down the chimney. Only he wasn't going to tell that to a nosy-parker doll.

'But I thought witches could do things humans can't — why didn't she just fly in through a window when the Sterns were here?'

'I don't know. I don't know, she's scared of humans, that's why; there's some sort of power *they've* got that witches haven't, and don't ask me what, I don't *know*. And anyway,' he snapped you're the nosiest person I've ever met! Oh my beak and tail, where's that Lifestone, she'll pull out all my tail-feathers if I go back without it.'

Lark didn't like to mention it, but he only had one tail-feather left. She was beginning to feel the merest bit guilty now... 'Hadn't you better, though? Come on, I'll show you the way,' she said, and led him quickly — so as not to do anything silly, like show him the Lifestone — out of the moonlit kitchen and into the flagstone passage behind. Just down on the opposite wall was a door.

'The dining-room, Mrs Stern forgot to close one of the shutters in here. She often forgets things.'

The house-agent had called the room *'la salle à manger'* but the Sterns had used it as the hub of the house. When it rained they ate in it (usually meals had been outside), the children painted in it, wrote in it, read in it, Tom hatched tadpoles and built model aeroplanes in it, and Sarah had had her zoo of lizards and mice, while at night Mr Stern cooked steaks on its open fire.

There was a lot of oak panelling, and opposite the fireplace was another set of doors, big double ones, and in the two other walls windows were set, one looking out on to the overgrown orchard behind the château, and the other on the park in front.

It was the one looking out on to the park that Mrs Stern had forgotten to close, but Skite didn't need telling. There was a table under the sill, and he hopped up squawking excitedly.

'Ho, ho, ho, another way out! Another way out, another way in, wait till I tell Ermyntrude! She can visit the toys and find the Lifestone herself. Hoo, hoo, hoo, who's the King of the May, who's going to have a great big dish of grass for his breakfast? Skite is, Skite's going to!'

'No, no, no, you mustn't tell her,' cried Lark in alarm. 'I know she means to catch me.'

Skite swore. Just his luck for everything to go

swimmingly, and then get a spoke in the wheel. But the doll had been kind. Once the witch got inside she'd

be thrust into that toybox, Ermyntrude's toy, awaiting Ermyntrude's pleasure. He gave in to his conscience.

'Climb on to my back and I'll fly you on to the sill.' He hopped on to the floor, crouching for her to get on.

Lark's stomach lurched thrillingly as they took off. 'Take me round the room, just once! You're so *soft*, it's like — like —'

'Flying.' Grumbling but flattered the goose swooped over the mantelpiece, plunged downwards skimming flagstone and rushmatting, then grinning at her squeals and gasps, zigzagged alarmingly across the room, just missing the ceiling, and for a grand finale zipped three times round the cornices.

'Oh lovely, lovely, Ermyntrude's so *lucky!*' They landed breathlessly on the sill, and Skite looked pleased.

'You balanced very well for a first time. Now when I've gone, you'll have to close up after me and slide down the table leg. Do you think you can manage?'

'Yes... Skite.' She wished he wouldn't go. 'Skite, I've been thinking, you must have some idea — what *is* it humans can do that witches can't, what's the power Ermyntrude's so afraid of ?'

'Oh my beak and tail, I don't know. Questions, questions, you mind that little brain doesn't burst out of that shiny wooden head of yours.' He pushed the window open with his beak, and balanced on the sill. 'I'm off. What's your name again?'

'Lark,' said Lark sadly.

'Goodbye, Lark,' said Skite and was gone.

She was alone again.

24

3

Ermyntrude woke with a snort; one look at Skite told
her all she needed to know.

'Bumpkin, fool! Come back without the Stone, have
you? Measly, mangy, half-witted skeleton, it's a doll —
the doll has the Stone!'

Hoodwinked. Of course. How else could you explain a
walking, talking doll? Skite felt peeved and rather hurt,
as though Lark had betrayed him.

'Geese aren't supposed to be clever,' he sulked, 'and
you starve me. How can I think on an empty stomach?
If you let me eat grass, I expect I'd be brilliant. Grass is
brain-food, everyone knows that.'

...Of course nobody in their right mind would give up
the Lifestone, he quite saw that. And the Lifestone

25

must be retrieved, he saw that too. And he would not, he absolutely would *not,* go down that chimney again after it.

'You'll have to go down the chimney again after it,' Ermyntrude said.

Skite set his beak. 'You can force me down there, mistress,' he said in a quavering voice, 'but you can't force me back with the Lifestone. You'll never be thin enough to come down after me, and I can stay locked in the château for ever and a day.' Astonished at his own daring he scooted along the roof out of range.

Ermyntrude thought fast — she was a very ancient witch, ancient as the hills round Lark's Castle, and once she'd been extremely powerful; but nowadays the most elementary magic seemed fraught with difficulties. Skite inside the château might be beyond her control.

'Silly, silly Ermyntrude,' she crooned. 'Ermyntrude wasn't thinking!' There was plenty of time, the first dew had scarcely fallen, and another little nap would clear her brain.

'Why doesn't Skittikins help himself to a woodlouse? Then he can scratch us up a lovely pile of grubs, and we'll think it all out over breakfast.' Without waiting for an answer she rolled over in her moth-eaten cloak, and started to snore again.

The first thing Lark did when Skite had gone, was cry. All the tears that had been mounting since midnight came pouring out, tears for the school days, the summer days, the games in the park she would miss, bitter tears for Sarah, tears for not being owned.

Though only a little while ago she had longed to shout, 'We'll come back, Sarah, we'll come back!' she knew it wasn't true; a chance advertisement at the start of the Easter holidays 'Château holiday very cheap' and Mr Stern needing a month of quiet to finish his book, when would that fitting-together of things happen again?

Of course lots of people wouldn't have thought it a holiday at all, what with the water to fetch from the well, the electricity breaking down two or three times a day, the furniture so dilapidated, the leaking roofs and the draughts. The only way you could keep food cool was in big stone jars, and at night you read by oil-light, sleeping on goosefeather quilts so as not to feel the lumpy mattresses, while out in the park the grass was waist-high and the orchard a wilderness. The Stern family had loved every overgrown, crumbling corner and so had Lark, but she'd never in a million years dreamed of being left there alone.

And how would she get out, how could she ever escape Ermyntrude? How in the world was she to get back to Battersea? In those moments she was learning to cry, life seemed a dreadfully lonely thing.

But it *was* life.

Life! Wasn't that always just what she'd wanted?

Unsteadily she climbed to her feet, and peered out over the park. The moon had sunk, gleaming fingers stroked the sky...all at once the wooden doll felt, not at the end of something but at the beginning, the start of some huge adventure.

Stretching up suddenly on tip-toe, she pulled the window to. Safe! At least for the moment. Then she

27

swung herself over the table, slid down the leg, and landed with a clatter on the floor.

Which way to go? The big double doors stood invitingly ajar. Her legs shook, and the floor seemed to stretch for miles, but she reached them at last and went through into the hall. There was the great front door, and Mr Stern's study facing her, but at the far end of the hall a large, very beautiful, stone staircase wound up and up round the inside of the tower. Lark stared, her heart pounding. She had no doubt at all her adventure lay up those stairs.

Skite was having a glorious time in the orchard.

The worms were the fattest, the beetles the tastiest he'd had in years, and under the appletrees (once you fought your way through the brambles) the grass must be the greenest, and tenderest in all France.

There was plenty for everyone, too. All around him sparrows and starlings, bluetits and chaffinches pecked, chattered, gobbled, and exclaimed; it was like being invited to a huge breakfast party and all at once Skite felt something he hadn't felt for years, he felt *young*.

He forgot about Ermyntrude, he forgot about the Lifestone, wandering hither and thither among his fellow-breakfasters, chattering, gobbling, and exclaiming back.

'Blast, blast, blast!' Reaching the foot of the stairs was one thing, climbing them another. Lark's legs were obstinately refusing to do what she wanted, which was to sprint upstairs two at a time to the top. 'Oh *move*, you silly wooden sticks,' she cried, and in a burst of temper plopped down on the second step, kicking her heels hard against the stone which hurt.

It was no good, they simply hadn't any practice. She'd have liked to watch morning steal over the

orchard while they got ready to move again, but the small windows cut into the tower were too high, so she sat on the step listening to the breakfasting birds outside, wishing she had wings instead of legs.

Of course, Skite ruminated on a full and happy stomach, it was many a moon since he'd had any grass at all. Ermyntrude had a horror of vegetables; she thought they made you soft, and she wasn't having Skite soft, so what with her snapping up all the grubs he scavenged, besides all her midnight feasts of lizards and toads, he never got more than a couple of stringy worms of a meal and maybe a woodlouse for pudding.

The grass was having a strangely rosy effect. He remembered the nosy wooden doll with a sort of rusty affection and he quite hoped Ermyntrude wouldn't roll off the chimney-pot.

It might be the sort of adventure that took her half across France, and over the Channel to Battersea. Lark knew all about magic carpets for they featured a lot in Sarah's games, and she had a pretty good idea that that's what was waiting for her up in the château attic; her legs were behaving wonderfully now, she gave a whoop of excitement as she reached the first landing. Three big bedrooms led off the corridor, and at the end where backstairs and corridor met there was an anti-quated bathroom with an antiquated bath which didn't work; but the adventure and the carpet were higher and her heart thumping all over again, she followed the curve of the balustrade and went on climbing.

The top floor hadn't been used by the Sterns at all. Sarah had met some bats there on her first day's exploring, and liked them no more than Skite did. Now suddenly Lark met one too — swooping down out of the rounded darkness of the tower it swung on to the stone balustrade, clinging upside down and staring comically.

'Hallo.' It was the first live thing she'd seen since Skite, but the bat simply squeaked in a mindless sort of way, turned a couple of somersaults and plunged up-wards again into the dark. She sighed. Obviously bats didn't talk to dolls, perhaps no animal did. Except geese. But Skite was a witch's goose, he might have been magicked...next time she saw him, she'd ask.

'King of the May, His Majesty Skite
Has just had a breakfast that's more than a bite
His stomach is full...' croaked Skite,
'But his head it is light,
Oh high as a kite
In flight
Is Skite!'

Ah, life was wonderful, the sun was wonderful, the wooden doll was wonderful, Ermyntrude was especially wonderful; look at the way she balanced up there snoring like a giant train! With a sloppy smile Skite tucked his head under his wing, and began to dream that high, childish voices were drifting through the morning sunshine...

They penetrated the third of his forty winks. With a startled squawk his eyes flew open, and swaying a bit, he made for a dense bramble bush from which to look. Five or six figures were prancing across the park, shouting and calling — the children from the farm, always up early; Tom and Sarah used to play with them, they must have climbed the gate.

...None of his business. He belched gently, and with the sun hot on his back, snuggled into the grass and began his forty winks again.

Voices...*voices*? Lark stood stock still on the top landing. Voices in Lark's Castle, when Lark's Castle was shuttered and closed? And they were up here on

31

the top floor, along the corridor and round the corner — somewhere down that corridor! Low, murmuring voices... She couldn't make out a word.

A skylight in the sloping roof made a pool of light on the floor, where landing met corridor. She crept to it, and stood there straining her eyes down the dark passage: beetles scuttled along the floorboards, a mouse hurtled past, and remembering (how long ago, a whole night ago!), Mr Stern's explosion 'Dragons in the wainscot!' she half-expected to see little green combed heads with curling red tongues pop out of cracks in the wall. None did, and anyway these were human voices, nothing magical about them except that they were *here*. She must find them, she must hurry, she mustn't make a noise in case she frightened or shocked them and they ran away.

Four doors she saw, led off the corridor; she went through them one by one. They were boxrooms, dark and small with one tiny window each that jutted out of the slate roof. In the old days they must have been servants' rooms, and they were in worse repair than anywhere else in the château: small iron bedsteads stood in each one, rusty pipes clung to the walls, cobwebs drifted in clouds from the ceilings; the dust along the skirtings was full of chipped paint and in one or two rooms the wallpaper had completely come away from the walls, and swung in huge floral arabesques to the floor.

And all the time she was drawing closer and closer to the voices.

32

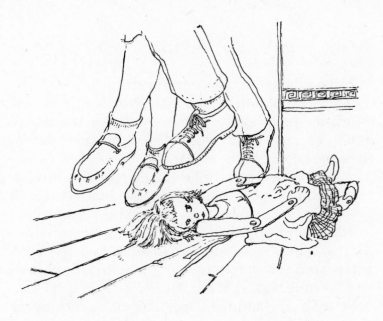

4

It was the end of the corridor but the corridor didn't
end, it turned a corner, and a black, yawning space
stretched away on Lark's right. Up it, like gusts of wind
the voices blew and drifted. She began to inch forward into the dark, her heart in her mouth, for the
floorboards here even under her small weight were
terribly shaky, as though no one had trodden them for
years.

Then she caught a word, leaping like a fish out of the
ripple of sound: another, and another, French, the
rough country French of these parts. Lark was actually
French herself, carved by a Breton peasant though she
didn't remember it, and bought at a country fair by

Sarah's mother before the little girl was born. *'Partis...'* she heard. *'Viendront plus...'* Gone. Won't be back.

'Nobody'd know,' a second voice urged.

'They're not ours,' said a third, clear and strong. Suddenly Lark recognised it, Philippe, the boy Tom used to tickle trout with. The farm-children! What were they doing in the château?

'...wish there was...' She couldn't catch Lotte's wish but Philippe spoke sharply to his little sister. 'Well there isn't, and if there was, you couldn't take it!'

What were they doing, but more important how had they got in? The farm lay just beyond the château gates, Tom and Sarah used to run across the park every day for milk, eggs, butter, cheese. They'd spent a lot of time with the farm-children, six or maybe seven of them, ranging from three to twelve, dirty and nice, red-cheeked in hand-me-down clothes, with no toys of their own except what they made, and many a time Lark herself had been played with by Lotte. Perhaps Lotte would wrap her up in a parcel and send her back to Sarah!

In her excitement at the thought, the little doll began to run into the dark towards the children. Slap, a wall loomed up to meet her and she crashed down, falling over a step; at the same moment echoes of the village clock pealed faintly through the château.

'Zut,' she heard Philippe through the wall, 'the school bus, we'll miss it!' A door was flung open above her, daylight hit the step.

'Come on, leave everything, we can come back later.' Winged feet, through a haze of little stars she saw them

34

fly over her head, and nimbly, lightly, knowing where to tread, hopscotch over the floorboards...and as the echoes of children rushing, jostling, laughing, grew fainter and fainter down the backstairs and died, she stumbled up the step and stood at the threshold of the vast castle attic.

Then she gave a sudden, great shout of laughter, the first she'd ever uttered.

Which was probably what woke Ermyntrude on the chimney-pot.

'Breakfast...breakfast,' she mumbed. 'Br - e - a - kf — where's that gormless knock-kneed goose? Skite! Sk - i - i - i - *ite,*' but Skite was slumbering sweetly, deeply, drunk as a Majesty might be on grass and sun in the orchard. 'Skite, you spineless —' With a cry of shock, Ermyntrude clutched her stomach. Her Lifestone, lost, she'd almost forgotten!

'Skite, Skite!' Not a feather to be seen, in the sky, on the rooftop, amongst the elmtrees in the park. 'Oh help, help! Help a poor lady who wouldn't say boo to a goose, help a sweet old witch who never did any harm. Agony, agony,' Ermyntrude wailed, 'bereft of my Lifestone, deserted by my trusty goose — trusty, my *broomstick.'*

'You haven't got one,' croaked a dreaming, drunken voice in the orchard. Ermyntrude, who was a bit short-sighted, not to mention deaf, peered over the rooftop in the wrong direction, to where half-a-dozen small figures were scrambling over the park gates; she thought they were hedgehogs.

'Lal, lal, lal,' floated up from the appletrees; she turned round and peered down the other side, where a

35

large white blob seemed to be resettling itself under a bramblebush.

'High as a kite

His majesty Skite...' sang the blob. Ermyntrude went purple. Drunk, the goose was drunk! He must have shovelled down mouthfuls of that lush green grass while she slept.

'Bereft,' she shrieked. 'Deserted — deserted and bereft.' He might be drunk for days, he might snore and croak for a week. Somehow or other (her knees turned to jelly) she had to get down there to wake him, or life and the Lifestone were lost.

'Unlucky witch,' she howled, 'oh ghastly peril...just a sweet old lady... Ah trust,' she rallied herself, 'trust to the drainpipe, Ermyntrude. Avaunt, ye last witch of Rezay, remember the rich witch blood of your forbears.'

With groans of terror, she unbuttoned her boots for the great descent.

Toys, toys, and more toys, a treasure trove of them scattered in heaps and piles, muddles and mounds, across the vast attic floor! With a cry Lark flung herself into their midst: skittles whizzed, a skipping rope snaked through the dust, balls rolled, bats tumbled...

On its own under the skylight, a tiny brass-and-leather trunk stood, and she rushed across to it, tripping over a mountain of bricks. Astonishingly, it opened with ease and inside, beautifully laundered, and protected by tissue against moth and cobwebs, were neat piles of the most exquisite little dresses in silk and satin, cotton and lace; handsewn every one, and looking as if they might crumble to dust at a touch.

She drew out the first with trembling fingers, soft white cotton stitched with fragile lace — and her size, she was sure it was her size. It couldn't hurt to borrow it!

Off came her smock, the precious Lifestone tucked in its pocket, and as carefully as she could manage with her unpractised wooden fingers, she put the white dress on. It didn't drop to bits, it reached the ground and it was beautiful. Gathering the skirt and humming in an odd, flat little voice she began to sway…

And then Lark was dancing, not very well, not well at all in fact, but round and round amongst tops and shuttlecocks, tiddlywinks and marbles, puzzles and playing cards, wooden boats, chessmen, clockwork

37

mice; there was a bald teddy-bear with glazed button eyes, there was a kaleidoscope, there were kites, there was a Noah's Ark full of staid little painted animals: there was a doll's house, a gollywog, a steam-engine, a jack-in-the-box, goodness only knows what there wasn't.

How astonished they must feel to see her, an ordinary-looking wooden doll cavorting in her borrowed finery. How they must long to do the same.

'Only wait, only wait,' she sang out as she hopped and spun, tripped, and picked herself up again, 'all my life till now I've been lying too, still and never answering, I've lain wherever I was put. Lifeless like you, and longing with every grain of wood in me to live — but wait, just you wait!'

She couldn't wait. Darting to her smock she drew out the Lifestone which glimmered in the morning sunshine, looking as pale and uninteresting as she knew it wasn't. For a moment she clenched it hard in her palm...then she lifted the lid of the Noah's Ark, and dropped it in.

A long, long time went by, several minutes at least, and Lark began to imagine the most awful things, mainly that the Lifestone had lost its magic.

But all at once a pale blue light began to glimmer fitfully round the Ark and there came a heaving and a creaking like old trees in a storm. The Ark began to swell and shrink, hardly noticeably at first, but swell and shrink like a pair of bellows, and on top, the little house trembled with the echoes of a strange concert starting up in the hull.

There were snorts, grunts, squeaks, cheeps; there was

38

baaing, roaring, miaouing, mooing, jabbering, neighing, barking, screeching all mixed up with a thousand other noises which weren't, it began to dawn on Lark, just sleepy or even a little bit disgruntled. These were the voices of animals up-to-the-eyes, and down-to-the-toe-nails outraged and annoyed.

She watched with dawning horror. Splinters of light were glancing off the Ark's roof and walls now, just as they had around her in the kitchen but these were dim little things, they seemed to stagger not leap, and they fizzled out mid-air; while with dreadful reluctance the door creaked up into its lintel, showing a rabble of bad-tempered animals on its threshold.

A plank swung down onto the Ark's deck. Grumbling angrily, an elephant lumbered down and made a beeline for the deckrail, where it sank to its hindquarters with a groan. 'Frightful, frightful,' it trumpeted in a quavering voice to the giraffe who was following.

'Absolutely disgusting,' squawked a pelican flapping down the gangplank after them. 'It's no good sitting there,' it added to the elephant, 'you know what's expected.'

'I'm waiting for my mate,' mumbled the elephant.

'Mate! mate! mate!' a hundred voices took up the cry as animals came pouring, blinking, stumbling out of the Ark, and there were shouts of 'Get along there, don't sit about, God won't like it.'

'I suppose,' said a cheeky-looking monkey, 'it *is* God giving the orders?'

' "Suppose", "suppose", you weren't *made* to suppose,' snorted one of the pigs.

'God or Noah, who cares? Orders is orders!' growled a

39

baboon; the monkey lost his tongue and fell into line with his mate.

'Noah's lost, you know,' the lady mole squeaked short-sightedly to what she thought was her mate, but was actually an owl. '*And* Mrs Noah, *and —* '

'Towhoo, towhoo,' the owl agreed mournfully. 'You're in the wrong place, where's my mate?'

'Mate! mate! mate!' cooed, roared, jibbered the rest.

'That's right, take your partners all,' shouted the baboon bossily. 'Sooner we start, sooner we stop. No call for talking, just lead with the right and quick march till the order comes to stop.'

'What a business, what a business,' clucked the hen to the cock.

'You there, *QUIET!* Round the deck two by two, *if* you please,' and round and round the grumbling cavalcade went, at a snail's pace (a pair of snails was actually leading the crocodile, though the crocodiles said they ought to be), panting with the exercise.

Breathless too, and crosslegged by the Ark, Lark watched. Any moment these animals must realise the wonderful thing that had happened to them — must break rank and come tumbling over the deckrail. Her smoothed, white, lace-and-cotton lap sat ready for the hordes of joyous animals to catapult into, but nothing of the sort happened.

Eyes fixed on the tail ahead, all desire to practise their new-found voices quenched, the jumbly procession wove in and out through the open door and round and round the outside of the little house. Every now and again somebody stumbled, or scratched, or sat, causing the ones behind to fall over him and the whole

40

line to collapse backwards like a pack of cards; and then they'd simply pick themselves up again and go on.

You couldn't imagine a more dismal, less inquisitive crowd if you tried, and suddenly Lark could stand it no longer.

'Oh do stop going round and round, you're making me dizzy,' she cried. 'You're alive, you silly things, come over the side and run about on the floor.'

'Run *about*?' gasped the hippopotamus.

'Was that orders?' one of the mice squeaked. 'Was it God?'

'Certainly not, keep going or I'll eat you,' growled the tom-cat; the baboon snapped like a terrier.

'*QUIET,* order, order! You there on the other side, none of your lip.'

Lark sprang to her feet, her short hair swinging furiously. 'And you stop being so bossy! Of course I'm not God,' she told the others, 'I'm a doll, I'm wood like you, and I'm alive like you — we're *alive*, don't you know what that means? We can jump and shout and climb and fly, we can do anything! Look at me.' She leapt into the air and landed in the splits, yelling 'Gadzooks!' as she'd heard Sarah do when she was being dramatic. Nobody lifted their heads from their snail-paced crawl.

'You're all a lot of sheep,' she shouted, 'going nowhere, same direction, same silly circles, nobody's even *looking*. Do something different, you don't have to do *that*.'

'Ah but we do,' said the monkey, 'we're creatures of no character.'

41

'No character,' brayed the donkey. 'Nose to tail, nose to tail!'

'Tail to nose,' giggled a squirrel.

'Tails and noses,' chorused the others.

'Orders is orders,' the baboon said sullenly. 'We was ordered to live, so we're living, but no more'n we have to and the sooner it stops the better.'

'But it wasn't an order, it was a — it was a magic invitation. It wasn't God, it was me, I thought you'd be glad.'

'*Fly*, who wants to fly?' sniffed the lady giraffe. 'Interfering upstart.'

'Don't worry, I wouldn't *dream* of wasting any more magic on you,' said Lark furiously. 'You can stop living this minute, you don't deserve it, any of you,' and she turned her back because she was afraid of crying, but they were all too intent on their aimless parade to notice. All that is, except for a kindly old lion who glanced across to say:

'There, there, don't take on lass, life's too much trouble d'ye see? Trouble and tears. Us don't want it. Give us back the sleep we're used to, there's a lass.'

Her eyes stung too much to answer. Snorting, she lifted the lid of the Noah's Ark and took out the Lifestone, which was hardly brighter than when she'd put it in. There was a sudden, wild scramble as the animals used their last minutes of life rushing to the door. The last snail scurried in and it closed with a bang.

'The worst lot of spoil-sports I ever met in my life,' she told herself forlornly, and she sat down to howl and then decided not to; there were plenty of other toys after all, and there couldn't be anyone else who'd refuse to live. Feeling hopeful again, she laid the Lifestone on the jack-in-a-box and waited anxiously.

Once more the blue lights jumped out, as feeble and small as gnats. The lid opened with the same grinding slowness as the door of the Ark, and with a weak cry of 'Bo!' the jack flopped over the side of the box: then he scrambled himself back in again and very half-heartedly repeated the performance.

Lark was so startled that she couldn't think of anything to say except 'Bo!' back, but after a few times of saying this, she began to get rather annoyed. 'We ought to start up a conversation,' she told him next time he came out. 'Now, what do you think —'

'No thoughts, no thoughts,' said the jack. 'A person of no character, bo!', and back into the box he scrambled again.

'You don't mean —' she gasped, 'you can't *possibly* mean you don't want to live either?'

'No! Bo!' said the jack, and back he went again. Without another word Lark picked up the stone, and drifting with it to another heap of toys, sat down sadly on the kaleidoscope. A moment later it began to tremble very delicately under her weight, and a dim blue spark fell into her lap.

Hardly daring to hope, she jumped up and helped it on to its end, for of course it had no legs. The kaleido-scope gave a shudder and there was the sound of a throat being cleared... Lark held her breath.

Nothing happened.

'Oh please, oh *please,*' she was getting very frightened by now. 'Please do talk to me!'

43

'No ideas,' croaked the kaleidoscope in a voice she could hardly catch. 'No ideas...a person of no character,' he said sadly after a moment. 'Shake me, and I fall into whatever pattern you call...no ideas...' and he fell silent again.

Lark was ready to howl in earnest when a huge black shadow fell over the skylight, and an enormous foot wearing a yellow and purple sock that needed darning (the big toe was poking out), came slithering down over the glass, searching for a foothold.

5

'Aha, milady Peglegs!'

A vast leathery face peered in through the skylight. Its yellow eyes were wrinkled with age and ill-temper, it had a hooked nose with a wart on the end, a bristly chin (and three or four more besides), and it wore what looked like a huge pink-and-turquoise potted plant for a hat.

'Aha, my fancy lady, outwit Ermyntrude would you? Keep the Lifestone and be queen of my toys?'

Lark, after the first shock, badly wanted to laugh. It *was* a hat. Ermyntrude was practically bald and almost the last bit of magic that remained her was to change her hats at will. To cheer herself for her great descent to the orchard, she'd put on a vast Easter bonnet trimmed with a cherry blossom and peacock feathers.

'Queen of my castle, queen of my toys?' she screeched. 'Nasty wooden doll, you *shan't* play with my toys, they're mine, mine, MINE!'

'I haven't the least desire to,' Lark said haughtily (it was easy to be brave this side of the glass). 'They're the most boring creatures I ever met.'

'Hoity-toity. Quite the thing, my Lady Fal-de-ral, in your frills and furbelows! Missing Sarah, are you? You know what's going to happen to you, my fine princess? You're going to wither away with loneliness, you're going —' Then Ermyntrude almost lost her toehold as the most brilliant idea occurred to her.

'Here's a little bargain, princess, for you with your brand new brain. Climb up the chimney with the Lifestone, and me and Skite'll fly you back to Battersea.'

'Wh-at? Over the Channel?'

'Over a hundred Channels. Skite is faster than the Concorde.'

'But — but *England*? Oh,' the doll began to hop on the spot, 'could he really find the way? Oh, when can we start, where is he, where *is* Skite?'

Drat that drunken apology for a feather duster. 'Mapping out the route even now, polishing beak and tail for the adventure. Climb up the chimney, princess, do.'

'But why can't I see him?' Lark plumped herself down again on a pile of bricks, which hurt. 'I want to hear it from his own beak. Suppose it's a trick? Bring him up here and we can talk through the skylight — I won't move till you do.'

46

And drat to Battersea and back that tricked-up know-all doll in her white lace frills. 'You start that climb this minute, Miss Frilla-bellil,' hissed Ermyntrude, 'or I'll — I'll —'

'Come down and fetch me?' Lark asked helpfully. The witch shouted six unmentionable things at once, then there was a shriek and the sound of a lot of slates dislodging. She disappeared from view.

Perhaps the wooden doll thought, she wouldn't so *very* much mind life being taken away again, once she was back with Sarah...and the Skite-flight to Battersea would be a wonderful adventure. But suppose Ermyntrude pushed her off, when they were out at sea? Well she'd float, that's all, she'd *float* back to England.

She kicked excitedly at a rubber ball and watched it sail high into the air; then it wedged itself in the rafters where two beams joined and made a corner.

But the corner was actually a shelf, and something was on it besides the ball; straining her eyes she made out a large wooden box smothered in cobwebs, its brass lock green with damp.

It was quite out of reach. And quite irresistible.

If only Tom's fishing-rod were lying about! Or a broom. There was a broom downstairs in the kitchen cupboard — Lark groaned, realising she could never drag it up two flights on her own. There must be something, *something* amongst all these toys that would bring the box down.

There was nothing. There were bricks. She picked one up, it was big, and she had to use both hands, it was heavy too: her throw fell a long way short, and next time she stood on the little leather trunk, but again the brick came nowhere within reach of the box.

And then she, too, had a brilliant idea.

There were hundreds of bricks, there were thousands of bricks, cubes, oblongs, cylindrical, diamond, bridge-shaped, T-shaped, half-moon shaped; there were plain wood, painted, picture and letter bricks, so why not build a castle, no, a *mountain,* a brick mountain! all the way up to the rafters and climb up the mountain to the box?

Ermyntrude was perched where for hours and hours she'd been perched — on the gutter. She simply couldn't make up her mind to go down the drainpipe.

The white blob looked quite big from here and much more obviously Skite. He was actually dreaming rosily of a succulent hillside he'd just been invited to share by a charming lady goose, and his chortles and snores wafted up in gusts to the gutter. Ermyntrude lost her temper. Stones, twigs, clods of earth, clumps of leaves, all the rubbish of the rooftop rained down on the unsuspecting goose.

'The prettiest beak in the world,' said he to his dream lady, as a dollop of mud landed on his own, 'and you shall be Queen of the May.'

Ermyntrude gave a howl. It had taken all day to get this far: her socks were worn out, her toes hurt, her knees were skinned and her gnarled old fingers torn to ribbons with clinging to the slates. Besides which she'd never gone so long without food or a nap in her life, and she didn't trust the drainpipe an inch.

'Too old,' she howled. 'Too old, too old. Ah, pity a sweet old lady, pity a poor old witch!' A crow flapped guffawing by, she shook her fist and her Easter bonnet fell off, fluttering down to the orchard where it melted. Sobbing noisily, she snapped her fingers for a black mourning veil, but instead a pink bobble hat whizzed out of nowhere and settled on her head. Even her hat magic was failing her.

Parachute, that's what she'd do. Her cloak would be a parachute, anything rather than the drainpipe. Teetering tremulously on the very edge of the roof she realised she couldn't possibly do it; she pitched forward and plunged.

A sea of appletrees came leaping up to meet her. Ermyntrude held her nose.

Lark's mountain was magnificent. She had seen a picture of the Pyramids long ago in Sarah's geography book, and it was built like that, except that the sides were stepped. Using a wooden truck she'd gathered bricks from every corner of the attic, and climbed up and down with them tirelessly: now at the very bottom of the last pile of bricks she discovered a bow-and-arrow set.

She drew an arrow from the quiver, it was twice as long as she was, but very light and fine, and perfect for poking at the box with. Using it as a balancing stick and carrying the brick that was to crown everything, she climbed her rainbow-coloured mountain for the last time; the bricks trembled, but held. Inch by inch she crept to the top, lowered the last brick, and scarcely breathing, pulled herself up on to that.

49

Then without meaning to, she looked down.

The attic floor tilted wildly; toys, bricks, oceans of colours heaved below her, she made a lunge at the box with the arrow — oh wonder, it moved! But beneath her feet the earthquake roared, it was going to swallow her, she made one last desperate thrust and the mountain caved: a dark weight came hurtling towards her, an army of colours and shapes attacked, she went down beneath them.

Lark held her nose.

Ermyntrude's cloak had proved a dreadful parachute, being so holey, but luckily she'd landed in an appletree. If she'd gone on falling without the Lifestone to protect her, she'd have had a pile of broken bones and most likely been dead.

But there she was, swinging by her cloak on a dangerously-bending bough. She snatched at an army of maggots struggling out of the bark, cramming them into her mouth while she thought about disentangling herself, then the bough broke and she landed with a crash in a bramble bush.

And once again the stillness of the spring evening was broken as children's voices tumbled, shrill and excited through the park.

The box had spilled its contents over the shattered mountain. Lark pulled herself painfully out of the rubble to look.

Toys — she could hardly bear it, four new toys!

If only it had been a magic carpet, she could have been chased all the way to Battersea by Ermyntrude on Skite (she and the carpet would win of course, but only just).

Instead there was this stout-hearted, wise-looking (his eyes looked so old) pottery horse, streaky with greens and browns as though paint had dropped on him and run down his sides; and all over him there was a network of tiny cracks, while the grooves where his tail had broken off were filled with the dust of centuries. In spite of her first disappointment Lark felt a rush of liking; she reached out and rather timidly stroked the flaring nostrils, the broad barrel chest, the wonderfully stocky legs standing so firm and foursquare...why, he must be hundreds, he might be *thousands* of years old!

And there were two dolls, a rag one rather homely and foreign-looking, with wide cheeks and a gentle expression stitched to her upturned eyes. Her hair was strands of brown wool, and she wore a red kerchief knotted under her chin and black knitted boots with buttons; her dress was a patchwork, little scraps of rag flowered and spotted, striped and plain, bright once and pretty, but threadbare now with an age of hugging.

The second doll, Victorian, though Lark didn't know it, was the prettiest thing imaginable with a sawdust body, and arms and legs and face of china: true there was a sour look to her rosebud mouth, but when she'd slid down the brick mountain huge blue eyes had opened and shut, and her cheeks were like rose-petals, and the nails on her fingers like tiny shells. How her small mistress must have loved her — yet the silver-green taffeta dress was as crisp as the day it had been made, and the golden curls had surely never been disarranged in their life. Had she ever been *played* with this doll, had she ever been cuddled and hugged and taken to bed?

Lark was growing wildly excited again, there was something *different* about these toys, they were older, much older than the others of course, but it was more different than that.

'They're breathing inside themselves, that's it, they're alive *inside*,' she thought, 'just as I've been, all these years. As if the life of the tree I came from was trapped in me, till the Lifestone brought it out.'

She rushed round to the other side of the mountain and found herself staring into a pair of long, hollowed-out eyes, the eyes of a toy too precious to be a toy for he was made of bronze. Or what she could see of him was, athlete's shoulders thrusting through the bricks and a bare left arm and a head, the head with its straight brow and no dent at the bridge of the nose, and his hair streaming as though he were running a race.

She tugged him free of the bricks, inch by inch. He wore only an olive wreath and sandals, and everything about him, every limb and muscle was singing with life — his mouth was so ready to laugh, it seemed impossible he wouldn't, and one sandalled foot was thrust high into the air, as if flat on his back he were still running.

He couldn't wait! Suddenly, staring into these holes for eyes she knew it, couldn't wait an instant more for life than he'd waited, however many years that was. Into his clenched hand she thrust the Lifestone and his laughter broke, actually broke like a huge gold bell through the château...

The whole attic blazed.

6

The eye-sockets became pools of changing greens,
never-endingly transparent, unplumbable as Greek
seas. Lark huddled trembling against the bricks. Could
God have felt like this, frightened and excited and
responsible when Adam first stood up?

The green crustiness of the athlete's skin was vanish-
ing, he grew deep brown-gold, but she saw only his
eyes...cloudy now, murky, sea-angry, sea-hungry; deep
and dark as cedars as he struggled at the brink of life.

Then the cleft chin shot up, the right foot snapped to
the ground, the runner's shout shook him from head to
toe.

'Great Zeus, *life*!' Down on one knee he sprang and

planted a kiss on Lark's foot. 'Mythical lady, goddess, nymph, *LIFE*!'

'Uh...' But the bronze boy was off, running, leaping, springing, round and round the edges of the attic, a blaze of gold in the fading blue lights of the Lifestone.

And then from another world, another century, she heard the farm-children's voices peal through the park and break like pebbles on the château walls. The farm-children, the children who had no toys!

How could they too, not fall in love with her wonderful discoveries? Bronze runner, pottery horse, rag doll and shining china one, she *must* bring them to life before the children found them.

'Oh, quick, quick, you,' she shouted. 'You please, whatever your name is.'

'Zis,' he was at her side in a bound. 'My name is Zis. Your command, mythical lady?'

'I'm not a myth —'

'Nor goddess, naiad, nymph, but you might be! Your command, magician?'

'But I'm not a — oh,' Lark took a big breath. 'Some children are coming, we have to hide, and we have to hide the others too, or the children might take them before they come alive. There's a loose floor-board, over there somewhere —' but already Zis was pushing the clay horse ahead of him, in the direction she was pointing.

Ermyntrude shook like a jelly.

She'd shinned up the nearest appletree, but the children had passed right under its boughs, and she was sure she'd caught that dreadful disease you caught from humans, love. If she had, of course, she'd become mortal, for the one thing the most powerful witch in the world can't do, is love.

She tested herself anxiously, but the children still seemed to her as snotty, noisy, and awful as children had always seemed, and Lark was the nosiest, cheekiest, most meddlesome creature she'd ever met, and Skite was simply a skunk, a drunk skunk.

...But where had the children *gone?*

One moment they'd been jostling up in the open air, next they'd rushed pell-mell down the cellar steps. The steps seemed to plunge straight into the bowels of the château, but Ermyntrude knew they led only to a huge underground room which, with its earth floor and rough stone walls was more like a barn than a cellar. There was certainly no inside door you could enter the château by.

Or was there?

They'd been so *quiet* all this time down in that huge great room. It wasn't natural. In fact it was fishy.

Very fishy. She had a perfectly horrible feeling...

There *must* be a hidden entrance in one of those walls, some secret door she'd missed.

'Anything at all in the whole, wide attic! If you could choose , Gerard.'

'Bow-and-arrows,' the boy next down in age from Philippe said instantly. 'My home-made one's not half so good. Your turn, Martine.' They'd played marbles, cards, tiddlywinks, the drum, they'd built and demolished a city of bricks, and Lotte had dressed and undressed the teddybear a hundred times. Now the

56

clothes were folded, the bricks stacked, and the toys ranged side by side in a corner, while they sat in the moonlight playing the game they always ended with, the game of If, or Suppose.

'The dresses in the trunk, all those little shoes and bonnets. They're so grand,' said Martine, 'they must have belonged to the doll of a duchess.'

'But what's the point when you haven't got a doll?' Lotte sighed. 'Oh I wish, I wish, I do, do *wish* there was a doll. A doll like Sarah's, any kind of doll, one like they have in the shop in Rezay.'

Lark trembled under the floorboards: it was musty and cobwebby, and there was funny smell of mushrooms, but it was a wonderful hiding-place. The rag doll made a cushion for the china one, but the pottery horse had been awkward: they'd been in the midst of wedging him when Zis had suddenly thrust her down, leapt in himself, and slammed the board down over their heads just as the children burst in.

'— And I wouldn't care,' she heard Lotte say now, 'even if it was a *terribly* old battered doll.'

'If I were nice,' Lark thought, 'I'd push up the floorboard and let them find us; Lotte could have the rag doll, or the china one (she can't have me). But I want to bring them to life, *I* want to play with them too! And — well. I'm not nice, I suppose.' She caught Zis's eye in the dark and felt sure he'd read her thoughts, but he only grinned that rather discomforting grin.

'I'll have the kaleidoscope,' another of the children was saying. 'You have to choose from what's here, Lotte.'

'And I'll have the Noah's Ark and the teddy and the jack —' began Suzy who was five.

'One thing, only one thing,' shouted the others.

'Well, the Ark then. There's lots of things in that.'

'Bwicks, want bwicks,' the smallest chanted, and 'Philippe hasn't chosen!' someone shouted.

'It's a silly game,' said Philippe. 'We can't take anything because whosever the toys are, might come back one day and want them —'

'But just *suppose*, Philippe!' He shook his head and they flung themselves on him, laughing and pummelling till he broke free, and laughing too, scratched his twelve-year-old head. 'Oh well, I'm a bit like Lotte,' he said, 'I'd want something that isn't here. Something old, something I felt had a lot of life behind it... I expect I'd just hold it and think of all the things that had happened to it before it came to me.'

Lark shivered again and glanced at Zis; he winked and she felt better. He wasn't going to give her away, but she couldn't help thinking how Philippe would like him. And the pottery horse of course.

Luckily just then the chimes of the village clock pealed faintly through the château, and the children sprang to their feet. 'Zut, my homework!' Philippe sprinted away across the attic floor, there was a wild scramble at the door and it slammed shut.

The children went rushing past, right under Ermyntrude's appletree again, and streaked away across the park in the moonlight; the second they climbed the gates, she shinned down, and began to dance round and round the tree stamping with rage and excitement.

They'd found a way into the château, they had, they had: they'd been inside the castle, *Ermyntrude's* castle, inside and playing with Ermyntrude's toys. There *was* a secret door.

Well, if they could find it, so could she, and once inside the Lifestone was hers for the taking — and all the long-lost toys; hers to pinch and torture, and wouldn't she make up for lost time.

Investigate alone, or rouse that feather-brained goose from his stupor? Two heads, feathered or not, were better than one, besides she might very well need some protecting.

'About time you got us out,' the china doll sniffed, 'my taffeta's *ruined*. Why didn't you lift the floorboard at once, that child was longing for a doll — she'd have taken me home and looked after me quite respectably I daresay. Hardly my dear Louisa, but beggars can't be choosers.'

'Ouff, a tongue to slay stallions!' exclaimed the Greek boy. 'Thank the gods for life, with it — or else the wooden magician. What is your name, magician?'

'Lark,' said Lark, trying to look as if she brought toys to life every day.

'Dost thou fly, dost thou sing, from what distant land do you come?'

'Battersea,' (she ignored the bit about flying and singing) 'but I was made in Brittany. In French my name's —'

'*Alouette,*' the wide-cheeked rag doll spoke shyly. 'My mistress used to sing *"Alouette, gentille alouette"*, my mistress is Katya, Katya Petrovna, have you news of her?' Her voice was grave and sweet and up-and-down, as if words travelled out of her mouth on a musical train, but her face fell when everyone stared so blankly. 'No, no...it is a long time ago, and in another country. I am Russian, my name is Masha, and,' she smiled at Lark, 'I am most glad to live.'

'Since we're being so free with introductions,' the china doll remarked, 'you may care to know that my name is The Honourable Arabella Hallowina Montmorency-Pellythew. *The* Montmorency-Pellythews. Hyphenated. Upper Highstandover, Wilts.'

The Greek boy gave a shout of laughter. 'Suppose you were a goddess, how should we address you? O

Divinity! O most sacred, noble, and Honourable-Arabella-Hallowina-Montmorency-Pellythew, Upper-Highstandover-Wilts —'

'Hush, hush,' murmured the Russian doll, for she'd had quite a religious upbringing.

'But Aphrodite herself was simpler!'

'Who's she?' Arabella demanded.

'Aphrodite, goddess of Love. So beautiful people need only look at her to love her.'

'True,' the pottery horse spoke in a warm deep bass. 'Aphrodite's fame spread even to China, where I come from. Ordinary people loved her, and of the simple nuggets of love they gave, she wrought things fine and beautiful — bigger than the stars. Then gave them back their love a hundredfold.'

'And that made them love her all the more?' Lark asked.

'And each other. For love breeds love, I do believe,' replied the horse. 'Small lady, I am of the T'ang dynasty, copied from a favourite hawking horse of the Empress Wu T'se-tien — T'ang, at your service.'

Then all at once Lark felt terribly shy. These four strangers, whose had they been, how had they come here, what did they actually *want*? Did they all have Batterseas and Sarahs to get back to? Yet how could that be, for now was *now*, the past was dead and gone.

Before she could make up her mind how to ask, the Greek boy gave a sudden roar of joy, catapulting himself into the air, then round and round the attic he went, handspringing, cartwheeling, leaping, somersaulting, in a whirl of movement that left the toys breathless.

'Oh, how I've longed to do that,' he gasped, 'how many times in the Stadium watched them leap and run and spring. If you could see them hurling the discus, like a man-made sun into the sky... Magician,' he dropped on his knees before Lark, 'life is a beautiful thing!'

'Oh I know, I know. I'm not a magician really, I'm only alive by luck,' and she told them how the Lifestone had landed in her lap. But at mention of Ermyntrude Zis's eyes grew dark and angry, Masha gave a cry of terror, T'ang pawed snorting at the floor, and Arabella picked cobwebs off her sleeve.

In a trice, everything fell into place. Ermyntrude, of course! How had they come to be here, from different countries, different centuries, except by some trick of hers? They hadn't been left by children of bygone days, but trapped by the witch, as Lark herself had been, to moulder in unloved silence for ever, here in the attic of Lark's Castle.

But *why?*

That was the great question. Why?

7

Everyone had gone very still, remembering old wounds at Ermyntrude's hands. It was T'ang who broke the silence.

'Traverser of continents, flouter of Time! My own acquaintance with Ermyntrude dates — what century are we now?'

'Twentieth,' Lark was glad of that deep bass. 'It's the 1970s.'

'Long gone! Nigh on thirteen hundred years then.' Only Zis looked unastonished, for he had known Ermyntrude at an even earlier date. The moon was shining in through the skylight now, white-gold and full, very high in the sky, and he was remembering centuries back just such a moon, this same moon blanching the temples of the Acropolis, remembering the youthful cry 'If I could run, Zis, if I could fly!'

A 'hrrrmph!' from T'ang brought him back to the present.

'Hrrrmph!' said T'ang. 'I will tell you what I know.

'Small lady, there was a time when Ermyntrude was hugely powerful. You say these days she rides upon a farmyard goose? In my time she used a metallic green broomstick of truly astonishing speed —'

'But she's — I mean, how could she *balance*?'

'In those days she was thin. Her immortality she owes to the Lifestone, indeed I have wondered if she was ever not alive, for her great favourites then were a wooden cat (toy for his child) carved by one of the slaves who built the Pyramids, and an ivory monkey snatched from the cot of a Mayan prince. Always the toys most precious and loved.'

'Why? Why those specially?'

'Love; Ermyntrude cannot abide it. She fears humans too much to meddle with them, but the love between children and their toys, that she must sunder ever and aye.'

'Ermyntrude's music,' Zis said bitterly, 'the crying of a child.'

'And what — what happened to the cat and the monkey?'

'Lost, their spirits broken by her tortures. And many besides, wrenched every one from his owner. Only we are here to tell the tale, we, the remnants of her collection.'

'Nay, the gems. We have survived, we have *life*!' cried the Greek boy. 'But unless we destroy her power we shall never be free.'

'If just we can find new homes, new children to love,'
Masha's voice quivered, 'for I know my dear Katya
Petrovna is long ago dead.'

'New homes, just what *I* said.' Arabella pointed
accusingly at Lark. 'If this person had only lifted the
floorboard, the farm-children would have taken us
home. Ermyntrude would never have dared snatch us
from their beds. And that's *my* dress you're wearing!'
She made a lunge at Lark, who dived under T''ang's
stomach and bobbed up the other side.

'It's not. I found it in the trunk!'

'My trunk. You don't think I'd come all this way
without my *clothes*? Not,' she added staring hard at
Zis, 'like some people.'

He grinned. 'Very warm, olive wreaths.'

'Hush, hush, Arabellushka,' the Russian doll soothed.
'Is beautiful, your dress, no need for have another.'

'Your grammar's awful,' said Arabella rudely. 'Anyway, it's mine and I want it.'

'Silly frilly thing. I wouldn't be seen *dead* in it!' Lark
peeled off the white lace dress and flung it at her feet,
then began to rummage furiously among the bricks for
her smock. T''ang rubbed his head thoughtfully against
his foreleg, then he trotted over to the china doll.

'Zis was teasing you earlier.' He frowned at the Greek
boy, who went red. 'Arabella is a beautiful name, and it
suits you. All the same you could take a leaf out of
Aphrodite's book, you know.'

'Pooh,' said Arabella. She glared at Lark, who glared
back. The smock was on again back to front, but if
Arabella wanted a fight she was ready. 'Pooh, silly old

goddess. Anyway, why?'

'Only that you are beautiful too, and people could love you just looking at you, if you'd let them. I would,' said the Chinese horse.

'Well they don't — yes, they do, they do!' A tear dropped quite suddenly on Arabella's little pointed boot. 'Louisa did, she put me in a big glass dome and said I was queen of the toys.'

'Oh, weren't you lonely?' Lark asked before she could stop herself.

'No!' And then the sour little face crumpled completely. 'Yes,' she whispered, 'Louisa had such a lot of toys, I think — I think really we bored her. Her mama and her papa were always away, she used to stand by the front door but they never came home, they just sent a new toy down in a carriage and she used to look at them and — and throw them in a corner.'

Everyone looked shocked. When Zis spoke, his voice sounded very uncomfortable. 'It seems to me that Louisa was not much loved herself, so how could she learn to care about you?'

'Well, she did, you needn't stand there looking stuffy and sorry for me!' Arabella whirled on them. 'She loved me just as much as any of your owners loved you — look what care she she took of me, look at my hundreds of dresses. And look,' she sneered at Lark, 'at your old smock, it's filthy and you've obviously only got one or why would you grab mine? Who's cared about you, I'd like to know. Magician, indeed!'

'Why, you horrible stuck-up —'

'Peace, peace,' the bronze boy leapt between them. 'There is only one foe, Ermyntrude. It is she we must

66

fight or by Zeus she will steal back the Lifestone, and no toy will be safe till the end of time. You, sir —' he bowed respectfully to T'ang, for there was something so wise-looking about the Chinese horse, 'you have the trustiest head among us, counsel us!'

Skite raised his eyes to Ermyntrude's with a dreamy smile.

'And you shall be Queen of the May,' he crooned. 'Ow — Ermyntrude!' He shut his eyes quickly, and dived back into the bramble bush.

'Ermyntrude, I'll Ermyntrude you!' She brought him down with a flying tackle. 'You drunken dolt, you rib-cage, I'll teach you to leave me up on a chimney-pot.'

'Ow,' screeched Skite flailing wildly in the folds of her cloak. 'Help, bats, nightmares!' It was pitchblack in the

cloak, and his head felt as if it had been hit with a sledge-hammer. One minute he was fathoms deep in roses with a charming lady goose, next he was being attack-ed, viciously attacked by a giant vampire bat who bore a remarkable resemblance to Ermyntrude. Or possibly three bats, it was hard to tell; somewhere in the dark he came across a vast leathery ankle which he bit, and the shriek that reached him turned his blood to ice.

'Up, you chicken's liver,' (which is about the worse thing you can call goose), Ermyntrude hissed. 'You pigeon-toed twig, you knock-kneed bag of bones, you carcass!' Skite staggered to his feet; his throat was parched, his head was splitting, and he could see three of most things but no bats; only one thunderously purple, impossible-to-miss Ermyntrude. 'Mercy, mis-tress,' he gasped, then he fell forwards on his stomach and everything went black again.

Ermyntrude bit her tongue, but there would be plenty of time for punishment when the Lifestone was hers again. She dragged him by the beak a little more gently out of the nettles, and on to a bit of newly-cropped grass; Skite stared at it miserably and belched.

'Walk!' said Ermyntrude. 'Keep walking till we get to the cellar. In a straight line,' for the goose had begun to weave dazedly in and out of the appletrees. 'I'll tell you why as we go...

'You see?' she finished as Skite tottered with immense care down the last two steps. 'We've got to find this other way in, time's running out.' As if to prove her words a hoarse cock-a-doodle-do! rang out across the valley, echoing through the cellar.

'Damn cocks,' Skite muttered. 'Never know the time

68

of day. Moon's still shining,' but he saw, oh he saw all right; and the second dew couldn't be far away, there was no time to lose.

He picked his fragile way across the earth floor to where a pile of logs was stacked against the far wall, and began to tap laboriously with his beak on each one.

'Not there, numbskull,' said Ermyntrude. 'In the wall. A secret spring, a button.' Just then one of the logs rolled down from the top of the pile, starting off another, then another. You couldn't see much but you could hear, and witch and goose made a dash for the moonlit entrance. A second later an avalanche of logs hurtled down over the place they'd been.

Skite gave a screech of terror, and clutched Ermyntrude: — a *thing,* a small, dark *thing* with sharp points sticking out all over it, was racing towards them over the logs. 'Help, help, fiends, a demon,' he yelped. A fierce pain shot up his right leg. 'Ow, murder, it's just stuck a horn into me! I'm getting out of here.'

'Don't be a goose,' Ermyntrude grabbed him with a quavering voice. 'It's just a — it's a — fiddlesticks, it's a hedgehog!' The hedgehog curled in to a ball and spun itself away into a corner, leaving Skite to gaze foolishly across the cellar at the wall that had just been uncovered. His eyes nearly popped out of his head.

The avalanche had revealed a hole large enough for a small person to squeeze through: it was the entrance to a tunnel, hollowed into the château's stone foundations, and it sloped steeply upwards.

'Quick, quick, hurry up Skite, it's the way, the secret way.' Ermyntrude was panting behind him like a huge pair of bellows. 'Ho, ho, ho, just you wait Lark Stern,

69

Ermyntrude's coming, Ermyntrude's on her way! You go first.'

'No, you,' said Skite. It was too much like the chimney all over again, even if it *was* up instead of down. 'I'll come behind, and push if you get stuck. And if you fall,' he added craftily, 'you'll fall on goose feathers.'

'Good idea,' said Ermyntrude. She barged past, and began to climb.

T'ang gazed round at the expectant faces. Lark and Arabella were studiously avoiding each other's eyes, but they were quiet.

'Well, it is clear we must break Ermyntrude's power, and the way to do that is by the Lifestone. I remember once, centuries ago, hearing her murmur in her sleep that should she lose it and a second dew dry ere she held it again, she must become mortal. When did the Lifestone fall in your lap, Lark?'

'Last midnight. I mean the night before tonight.' As if she could ever forget it.

T'ang beamed, 'And what would the time be now, I wonder?'

'Midnight again?' Arabella came out of her sulks.

'Later. Approaching cockcrow,' Zis said, and at that moment the same hoarse cock-a-doodle-do! that had so startled Ermyntrude echoed through the attic.

'That's rather a peculiar cock, you can't rely on it,' said Lark. 'A big black rooster from the farm, it crows at all sorts of hours.'

'Still, time's going on,' T'ang said thoughtfully. 'Dawn and the second dew won't be long. As long as we're in the castle we're safe. Lark has the Lifestone —'

'She ought to share it, we *all* ought to guard the Lifestone.' Suddenly Arabella rushed at Lark and tried to prise it from her fingers. 'No, it's mine!' Lark landed her a punch on the chest and, eyes flashing, backed away across the attic.

Arabella went for her; before anyone could move she had Lark by her round button nose and the two dolls were on the floor kicking, writhing, tearing at one another.

'Think you're so clever, Miss Wooden Sticks? We'll see how clever you look without your precious Lifestone!'

'You're a spoilt, horrible, selfish pig,' Lark shouted. 'And I'm going to find a way to make you *dead*.'

The words were no sooner out of her mouth than she could have bitten off her tongue. Across the attic Masha burst into tears, T'ang pawed angrily at the floor; Zis gazed at the moon through a marble, whistling some sad, archaic tune under his breath.

'I — I didn't mean it,' she stammered. The Lifestone slipped from her fingers, she watched it roll away among the bricks.

Arabella pounced. '*I'm* going to guard the Lifestone now, you obviously can't be trusted.' She swung round challengingly to the others. 'You heard what she said, she's not a responsible person, well *I'm* going to have some fun now,' and she ran straight to the first thing she saw, which was a damp, rather faded Catherine Wheel lying by itself in a corner. Lark was too sick and ashamed to look, but there was a tense silence among the toys as Arabella laid the Lifestone on its coils. Was something going to happen?

Whizz, whee, phoo, out sprang the magical blue lights, glancing and dancing through the air.

71

'Oo!' sighed the Catherine Wheel, 'Ah,' moaned the Catherine Wheel, 'if only you knew how I've waited for this!' She wriggled and writhed, and stood herself up, then she began to roll herself along the floor.

'Out of my way, out of my way,' she cried, 'Ah, how beautiful I shall be, I am the Queen, the Queen! These piddly blue sparks will have nothing on *mine*, watch me, watch me, my glory is coming!' Faster and faster she rolled, round and round the attic, and then she caught fire.

Back sprang the lights into the Lifestone, and whoosh, up in the air leapt the Catherine Wheel, spinning, whirling, loosing a million multi-coloured stars from her tail. 'See me, see me,' she cried, 'I am beautiful, I am glorious, I shall reign for ever and ever!'

The toys clung together in the middle of the floor, stunned. There was nothing haunting or magical about this storm of stars, none of the heart-stopping beauty the Lifestone showed at work; the colours were harsh, garish, the little stars pricked at you spitefully as they fell, and between her cries the Catherine Wheel spluttered and gasped in a horrifying way,

'Worship me, quake at my endless magnificence!' and indeed it seemed she must for ever leap, and bound, and scatter, among the rafters above their heads. Then the firework gave a sudden frightened squeal.

'Ah! Ah, what is it — what — I am falling,' she gasped, 'falling... Is it true, is it death? Queen of nowhere? Sinking, catch me,' she sobbed, 'dying, I am dying!' One by one the harsh little neon stars went out, there was a dull fizz, a sputter, and a charred socket fell to the floor, all that was left of the Catherine Wheel.

Nobody moved, Arabella was trembling all over. Zis watched Lark. The wooden doll had gone pale as the moon after her terrible utterance: paler still she was now, at this swift, appalling, life-and-death. At last — her legs moving like clockwork beneath her — she walked over, picked up the Lifestone and took it to T'ang.

'But Arabella's right, I'm not a responsible person,' she said in a low voice. 'You keep it please.' The pottery horse turned away. 'No, Lark, it's not for me.'

Like a sleepwalker she came to Zis, stared into his green eyes. 'Please.' He shook his head, the unruly hair flying and springing in the moonlight. 'I've nowhere to keep it, nymph.'

'In your curls.'

'No.' The bronze boy spoke quite gently. 'It came to you, it is yours. And you must be responsible.'

A sound like a little moan came out of Lark; she put the Lifestone in her pocket.

'Ahem,' T'ang cleared his throat. 'Well, I was, ahem, about to suggest a moment ago that to while away the time we should each tell the tale of our capture. And as Arabella,' he gave the china doll a nice smile, 'has already told us something of her life, perhaps she would begin?'

Arabella stared at her boots. 'Nothing to tell. Anyway, I know you don't really want to know.'

'Ah,' Masha rushed over and gave her a hug, 'we do, Arabella, we do!'

'Pooh.' To her horror Arabella found herself on the verge of tears; she had never been hugged in her life. 'Pooh. Well. Oh dear. Bother!' She wiped her nose on her taffeta sleeve. 'Well...one day — one day Louisa got into a temper, she said I was too perfect and she picked up the glass dome with me in it, and smashed it on the floor. And I was so happy! I thought, she's going to pick me up, she's going to play with me, and she *did*, she nearly did — only just then her nurse came in, horrible red-faced thing, and she said "Louisa, I've a surprise for you, your mama and papa have driven all the way from London to see you and they're waiting below in a carriage," and Louisa ran out of the door, and Ermyntrude flew in through the window and — snatched me!'

'Ancient Rhea,' Zis ran across the room and took her hand, 'that's a sad tale. But you're among friends now, Arabella, you'll find a new home, a loving child —'

'And your dress'll get worn and scruffy like mine. Sarah,' Lark nearly choked, 'Sarah would love you.'

Arabella didn't speak, but she darted a 'let's try again' look at Lark that only the wooden doll saw. Zis turned to T'ang.

'Tell us your tale, T'ang horse,' he said.

'Ah.' It was the first time they had seen the pottery horse look sad. 'My tale... I was the favourite toy of a little Chinese boy, but the dread Yellow Fever swept the land, and Ssu-ma, my small master died. As is our custom I was placed in his tomb, a room dug many feet below the ground, placed in his hand so that when he awoke in the Happy Beyond, he would not be afraid, for I should be there for him to play with.'

'Ugh, weren't you frightened?' Lark asked in a horrified voice.

'Frightened, why? There were so many pottery figurines with me, copies of Ssu-ma's friends, his family — I was happy at the thought of spending forever with the child I loved.'

'Even in a tomb?' Zis looked disbelieving.

'Even in a tomb,' T'ang said serenely. 'The tomb was a waiting place. Ssu-ma was a loving child, bound, inescapably bound for the Happy Beyond, and would he not take me with him? How should I be frightened or lonely?

'Well, as his father and mother, sisters and brothers bade the little boy his last farewell, a dreadful commotion broke out over our heads — horses neighing, squealing, stamping their hoofs, shouts of the charioteer, wheels grinding and spinning in the mud. The family ran up the steps, out of the tomb into the open air leaving the door to the vault ajar...and in those few seconds Ermyntrude swooped down on her metallic green broomstick, snatched me out of Ssu-ma's hand, and bore me away.'

There was a little silence.

'Oh T'ang! Poor T'ang,' Masha rushed across and flung her arms round his neck; the Chinese horse blew his nose rather noisily.

'And Ssu-ma,' Arabella murmured, 'waking without you.'

Lark felt too shy to hug T'ang, but she went over and stroked his mane. 'At least Sarah's *alive,* and I know where she is, and somehow or other I'll get back to her,' she thought fiercely. 'Poor T'ang...I'm lucky.'

Then Zis who had suddenly gone very still, said 'There are strange noises coming from somewhere beneath us, quite far beneath us.' Everyone held their breaths.

Scratch, scrabble, slip, grunt came up to them, very muffled, very indistinct, very far away...

8

'I am most sorry!' Masha was clinging to T'ang, unable to stop trembling. 'I think I am not brave, but…is it not Ermyntrude?'

'Nonsense,' said T'ang as cheerfully as he could. 'It is nigh on fifty years since she entered the château and that by way of the chimney — how should she now find a new way to enter?'

'Perhaps it's the farm-children come back,' said Lark, but she didn't really believe it.

'In the middle of the night?' Arabella looked almost as frightened as Masha. And there it came again, scrabble, scratch, slip, grunt, and sometimes scrabble, scratch, slip, grunt, squawk.

'Rats. Rats or bats,' said Zis, but inside he was thinking, 'The farm-children, how did *they* get in?'

'Rats, ohrrrr!' Masha shuddered again, but she looked a little brighter. 'Only that it be not Ermyntrude — oh, such a fear I have not felt since my first time to see her.'

'Where was that?' Zis said quickly; like T'ang he felt that the longer they remained in the attic, the safer they would be.

'In the ballroom of a Russian palace. We have many palaces in St. Petersburg.' She paused to listen but all had gone quiet below. 'Go on,' urged Zis.

'Ermyntrude flew in on the goose Skite, through a window very high among the marble columns. The ball is over, the dancers gone — and such a fear I have feeled, for she looks very terrible...seeking, seeking. One chandelier burned still, and she find me where I have been kicked by a dancer, under a chair of gold brocade.'

'Ooo,' Arabella gasped enviously, 'you went to a ball?'

'My mistress has taken me. She hid me in her bodice.'

Lark's eyes popped. 'But — she was grown-up, your mistress? Going to balls?'

'No, Katya Petrovna have fourteen then,' Masha's eyes twinkled. 'She put me in her bosom for to *look* grown-up. Her old nurse has made me out of many rags when Katya was very small, she had dolls more beautiful but I was everywhere taken with her.

'It is her first ball, her hair has been wound all day in rags and now she have a thousand of curls...and I remember there is a sadness that night in me to watch her dress, a sadness quite sudden, never I felt before:

77

that children grow and will leave us, for never we grow with them.' She gave a little sigh.

'The tears of things,' Zis murmured. 'Don't stop.'

'Well, but Katya's eyes are shining like two blue stars, she wears a dress of white organza and stockings of silk, and I too am going to the ball, I can peep over the top of her bodice! And the little bells ring in the snow, and the sleigh bears us, her mother and her father and her sister wrapped all in furs, right to the steps of the palace.

'What a staircase, you think it will lead to the Czar! All whites and gold, and trees in pots, and little boys run with goblets of silver, and wine like evening sun. Such medals, such braids, such feathers and jewels and silks, diamond lights, and fine young men in red and blue and gold; and Katya's feet go tapping, tapping, for the music is playing so you cannot stay still.

'No sooner we enter the ballroom, a young cadet bows for permission of dancing, and away we go, flying, dancing, laughing. He is dark and bold, and not so old, sixteen or seventeen — and she! Is this little Katya who blots her schoolbooks? In one turn of a mazurka, she is in love!

'Ah, do not laugh, my friends,' Masha smiled tenderly at the toys, 'love when you have fourteen is very serious. Soon she runs behind a curtain and takes me from her bodice — you see, she wants to be honest! So she ties me to her bustle and on they dance, for Ivan Ivanovitch will not let her go till the ball is over, and tomorrow he will call on her family, take tea from the samovar — but me! I have fallen from her bustle long before, many feet have danced over me, and I am spun to rest at last beneath the gold brocade chair.'

'And then Ermyntrude came in...' sighed Arabella.

'And Katya, didn't she notice? At the end didn't she notice? Didn't she ever notice you'd gone at all?' asked Lark.

'She was in love.' Masha smiled, then she gave a little sigh. 'Later came the Revolution to my country, and families like the Petrovnas have been wiped away; some there were who escaped, and I hoped...Ermyntrude has many times tortured me with tales... Oh,' she ran suddenly to T'ang and buried her head in his wither, 'can anyone to tell me, has Katya Petrovna been shot?'

'I'm worn out,' Skite groaned; he wished to goodness he'd never suggested bringing up the rear. Nine times Ermyntrude had slipped and nine times they'd slid all the way down to the bottom.

'Almost there this time,' Ermyntrude panted, 'one more heave, come on Skite, push.'

'And I've got a splitting headache;' he gave Ermyntrude's bottom a half-hearted nudge, there was another gigantic grunt, she heaved, and arrived.

She sat down, swinging her legs over the rim, and peered back down the tunnel waiting for Skite to emerge; there were little ledges hollowed into the stone to put your feet, but it had been wet and very steep, and goose and witch were filthy (not that you could see).

'Now where?' Skite demanded, flopping down beside her.

'Give me time to *think*!' snapped Ermyntrude. 'We must be *somewhere*.'

'In a cupboard.'

'Just what I was about to say.'

'So there must be a door.'

'Just what I —' It was pitchblack. 'Er...where?' Skite sat up, startled; it was the first time he had ever heard Ermyntrude unsure of herself. Could the loss of the Lifestone be affecting her sense of purpose?

The cupboard was quite small, he found a wall and began to tap vigorously with his beak; then he tripped over a broom. The door burst open and they fell out with the most enormous crash, onto the flagstone passage by the kitchen.

T'ang gently nuzzled Masha's hair, she wiped her tears on his mane.

'I am most sorry, most sorry!' she whispered: and then everyone leapt to their feet. A dreadful crash from somewhere beneath them shook the château from top to bottom.

Ermyntrude picked herself up and tried to think. She felt curiously weak, and the thought of a tussle with the wooden doll unnerved her. Well, she'd let Skite do that, she'd merely come up behind and snatch the Lifestone once he'd got it.

'Now if I was Lark Stern,' she said to herself, 'I'd think we'd come up the backstairs, so *I'd* go down the front ones. So *I'll* go up the back ones, and let Skite meet her the other way!'

Zis covered the attic floor in two long bounds, put his ear to the door. 'Footsteps! Ermyntrude's. She's coming up the backstairs!'

The toys froze, everybody looked at T'ang. Lark's

heart was beating so fast she thought it would jump out of her chest.

'Let us go and face her! There are five of us. T'ang and I will charge. I'll take Ermyntrude, you sir, the goose, and the nymphs must run between us.'

'Where to?' Arabella quavered.

'The window,' said Lark. 'The window I let Skite out of. But,' she stared at Zis fearfully, 'oh what about you?'

'We are fleet of foot, and strong, never fear — besides, the second dew must be almost upon us. If you can only escape with the Lifestone, Ermyntrude's power is broken.'

'And then?' whispered Arabella frantically. 'Shall we go to the farm and bang on the door?'

'No,' said T'ang, 'wait!' They could all hear the steps now, slow and heavy as Ermyntrude lumbered up the first flight. 'Why risk a meeting with her, better far we all leave together by the front stairs. Come — Masha, Arabella, we will start. Zis, will you take Lark?'

'He doesn't need to,' Lark began indignantly. 'I came up on my own didn't I?' She felt Zis's cool eye on her back. 'I'll come with Zis.'

'Then let us go.' The bronze boy pushed the attic door and it swung open; Ermyntrude's footsteps were growing ominously near.

'Zis, set Masha and Arabella on my back.' The boy swung the startled dolls on to T'ang's back and the pottery horse set off for the front stairs at a gallop.

'Quick, Zis!' but he grabbed her arm. 'Nay, she'll catch us up, catch us from behind, or the goose will. There is one chance,' and he pulled her back behind the door just as Ermyntrude's heavy steps mounted the landing.

'Cooee, coocoo, Skittikins! Have you got the little wooden horror by the beak?' she called. Skite, halfway up the front stairs where he was resting, sprang to his webbed feet and got the shock of his life. A white pottery horse was rounding the bend of the spiral staircase at tremendous speed, and clinging to his back were two terrified dolls — he must be dreaming!

T'ang was almost upon him when Skite dived off to the right through a gap in the balustrade, and shutting his eyes to banish the fearful vision, plunged straight upwards through the well of the staircase; up, up, like a comet until he hit his head on the dome of the tower, grabbed wildly at the rickety chandelier and swung there, dizzy and trembling, refusing to open his eyes. Somewhere along at the end of the corridor, he could hear Ermyntrude chortling and calling.

'Peck her to sawdust, Skittikins dear, give her a taste of your nice strong wing — steal my darling Lifestone would you, Lady Peglegs? Lifestone, Lifestone, Ermyntrude's coming.'

Silent as mice Lark and Zis clung to each other in the dark, as nearer and nearer Ermyntrude came, lumbered up the step, and stood on the threshold of the attic. Then out leapt Zis, and using all his strength, gave Ermyntrude an almighty shove from behind, pitching her forwards on to the attic floor and slamming the door fast. Quick as a wink he dropped to his knees, and Lark leapt on to his shoulders.

'Lock it! And bring the key.'

'I'm trying,' Lark panted, but the lock was stiff and on the other side they heard Ermyntrude stagger to her feet and like a maddened bull, make a rush at the door. 'Crunch!' just as the key turned. 'Crunch!' again.

'Bring the key, and *run!*'

Down the corridor like the wind they raced, skidding round the corner to the head of the stairs. Above them Skite opened his eyes, blanched, and shut them rapidly. Then they burst open again — there went the doll, the wooden doll Lark, and very likely the Lifestone too, getting smaller and smaller as she raced with Zis, round and round the inside of the tower, escaping before his very eyes.

'Lark,' he squawked, lurching violently on the chandelier. 'Lark, stop!'

'Keep running,' hissed Zis between his teeth. Down and down, round and round, they galloped, slithered, leapt, fell: one flight, two, they had reached the bottom and the hall.

'That way,' panted Lark, veering to the left. 'Oh, thank goodness, the doors are ajar,' and racing across the room they saw that the window, too, had been unlatched.

'Oh T'ang, wondrous T'ang!' Zis laughed aloud, and then he leaped, an astounding leap, so high and light and timeless Lark thought he would never land; but land he did, lightly on the table top beneath the sill. Then he dropped to his knees and stared — Lark, Lifestone, Ermyntrude, all the excitement of the chase forgotten.

'Daybreak. I never thought to see it again!' Daybreak, younger than sunrise, renewing of the world.

'Zis, me, what about me?' She had swarmed up the first bit of the table leg, and stuck; he reached over and swung her up.

'Look!'

Together they stood staring out over the park; Lark was a town-bred doll and she had never seen it before. She would never forget this first. Navy blue was scarcely an echo, and palest violet had grown into no light at all, not pink, not orange, nor green, nor gold...no-light was the promise of all light to come, while the waiting world held its breath.

Then gold stalked up over the horizon, and a line of hoofprints was clearly visible across the dew-soaked grass.

'The second dew,' breathed Lark. 'It's come!'

84

9

Skite was having a terrible battle with himself; at the
other end of the château he could hear Emyntrude's
screams turn to sobs of self-pity. 'But not tears,' he told
himself, 'not real ones.' In two hundred years he had
never seen her cry.

And a terrible two hundred years it had been, what
with the raids on children's toycupboards, the tortures
she'd inflicted on her captives: and now she couldn't get
to her old favourites, she tortured him instead.

'Cruelly, cruelly, getting so fat and making me take
her vast distances on no grass, and precious few
woodlice! And the names she calls me, the kicks and the
pinches, the aches, and the pains, it's a wonder I've

a tailfeather left.' Only the fear of the Great Beyond had kept him with her, and he was very ashamed of that.

Well, now he was free; there was no reason at all why he should rescue her. He could swoop down the tunnel, at a pinch climb the chimney, better still fly out Lark's window. He could, and he would! He'd leave Ermyntrude to moulder in the attic, find the wooden doll, and they'd live happily ever after with the Lifestone. He stood up resolutely on the wooden chandelier, wobbled, and sat down.

Ermyntrude...bereft of her Lifestone, bereft of her favourite toys, and now bereft of him.

What harm could it do to let her out? She could spend her last days repenting at liberty and who knew, find another goose.

'I will,' he thought. 'And if I don't find the wooden doll I'll just fly away and die at a ripe old age in some quiet little farmyard with my feathers on. I'm old enough to stop being frightened of the Great Beyond.' So saying he dived off the chandelier.

'Skite, my love,' called Ermyntrude as he flapped along the corridor, 'is that my dearie duck, is that my darling goose? Get me out, my sugar bones, and we'll have the Lifestone yet!' Sadly Skite pulled out his last tail-feather and picked the lock. There was a click as it turned.

Bang, she flung open the door so hard he keeled over, stunned. 'About time too,' she screeched, 'leaving me to fight an army of toys on my own. Oh, your Miss Nosy Parker Peglegs made plenty of use of the Lifestone while you were getting drunk in the orchard, there's a

whole army of toys, a whole avalanche attacked me —
and *you* let them escape!'

'I — er —' Skite began feebly, but his voice had a
definite pipe to it and there was a bruise the size of an
egg on his crown, and he wished Ermyntrude wouldn't
stand on her head.

'It's not a bit of good, Ermyntrude,' he gulped, 'I'm
not coming with you. You can chase the Lifestone on
your own.'

'You — you're — *what?* Don't you know what it
means if we don't get the Lifestone back?'

'Yes, it means you become mortal and I die in a
farmyard with my feathers on.' He ducked and tried to
run, but she grabbed him by the scruff of his neck.

'I'll deal with you later,' she told him frogmarching
him grimly down the corridor, 'but you're coming with
me and we're going to find the Lifestone if it's the last
thing we do.'

'I expect it will be,' Skite sniggered. *'Ouch!'*

Zis and Lark followed the hoofprints across the park,
through the neck of trees at the gates, and broke out on
to the road. It was surprisingly cold, a cool fresh dawn
on hand, but low-lying mists heralded a hot day:
through them, they made out the shape of the farm-
buildings and headed for them, running very fast.

'This way,' Lark panted, 'the farmhouse is this way!'
They wriggled under the gate, disturbing a large brown
dog who barked, then subsided into his kennel. And
then Lark cannoned straight into the black rooster.

He was so startled he let out a crow that galvanised
Ermyntrude at the top of the tower staircase. Without

a by-your-leave she leapt onto Skite's back, gave him an almighty kick, and they took off shakily for the descent. Lark simply ducked and ran on, for she could see T'ang, Masha, and Arabella shivering on the front doorstep.

'Oh, thank goodness,' said Arabella. 'We were so afraid you wouldn't come!' Masha ran forwards and gave Lark a little hug.

'I have banged on the door with my hoof,' T'ang said, 'but to no avail. What happened?' Zis told him. 'That was well-thought of,' the pottery horse said, and the bronze boy looked pleased. 'But I wish these children would open the door, I do not much care for this Western climate.'

'Well...' Lark's heart did a dive. She scuffed the ground with her toe. 'Well, I suppose I should be getting along, really. I've...quite a long way to go.'

'Larkushka, you do not stay?' Masha was dismayed. 'You do not stay for Lotte? For even so little a while?'

'No. I've a feeling if I don't go now, I never will.'

'You really *are*? All the way back to — er where?' Arabella asked.

'Battersea. Yes.'

'Yes. Battersea.' The china doll couldn't resist a little sniff. 'How?'

'I haven't quite worked it out yet,' said Lark. 'Walk I expect. Or swim. I expect I could learn.'

'Larkushka, I am sad.'

'I'll miss you.' Arabella looked embarrassed.

'We all will,' T'ang said, 'you gave us life. This grey curtain is thick, you will lose yourself — stay a little.'

Zis said nothing. Lark shook her head, and turned to

him awkwardly. 'Goodbye, Zis. Thank you for the last bit...for everything...for daybreak.'

'I will come a little way with you.'

'Zis, you will not find your way back!' T'ang exclaimed.

'I am not coming back. I go to seek the land of my gods. Will you not come, T'ang horse?' The Chinese horse simply stared. 'Do you not know that accepting to be owned again, you must lose your life? And you, Arabella, you too, Masha. And you, Lark, on your way to Battersea, the Lifestone will not help you then.'

'I know,' said Lark. It was as if she'd known it from the beginning. 'I've...thought about it. But I love Sarah, you see.'

T'ang looked at them both for a long moment, then, 'I have been too long without a master,' he said gruffly, and he banged once more on the door. It flew open.

Two children tousled with sleep, a boy of about twelve and a little girl of five or six stood on the doorstep in their pyjamas, staring at the toys. Then Lotte dived forward and scooped up Masha and Arabella.

'Oh Philippe, it's a dream!' she cried. 'Oh, they're so sweet — and that's, why, that's Sarah's doll.' She reached for Lark, who was down the steps in a flash. Zis leapt after her.

'Mais qu'il est ancien, ancien,' Philippe was stroking T'ang with a look of wonder.

'No dream,' cried Zis. 'And those toys in the attic, they belong to no one, they'd be glad of a home. T'ang, farewell old hawking horse, sweet rag Masha; beautiful Arabella, fare you well!' But the toys, long to as they might, answered not a word, for they had consented to

89

be owned and would never speak again.

'Goodbye,' cried Lark. 'Be happy. Oh, be happy!' and then from the direction of the park, the most dreadful cackles and squawks cut through the mist. It was Skite, protesting violently as Ermyntrude whipped, urged, kicked, pinched him along.

'Ermyntrude!' Zis turned pale. 'And the dew not dry upon the ground. Come,' he grabbed Lark's hand. 'I don't know where, anywhere, just run, we must run and

keep on running, we must lose them till the grass is dry.'

Lark felt as if everything inside her had turned to ice. She took Zis's hand and kicked her wooden legs into life again; under the farmgate once more they ducked, then back on to the open road. Far away behind they could hear Ermyntrude's bellows mingle with the goose's shrieks...

Skite could see almost nothing, for the mist had descended like a blanket. He flew a few yards bumped into a bush, alighted on the grass and waddled a few paces, then urged by Ermyntrude's heels, rose once more and crashed into an oak tree; he plummeted to earth like a stone, with Ermyntrude clinging on for dear life.

'You're not the goose I used to know, there was a time you'd have taken a little mist in your stride,' she grumbled.

'No,' Skite gasped, 'I'm not. We're both not. We're getting old. Time to settle down.' He thought longingly of his farmyard.

'Nonsense,' Ermyntrude did her best to sound brisk. 'All right, we'll go on foot till we're out of the park, then you've simply got to ferry me again. Once we're out of the mist and airborne, we won't be able to miss that army of toys.'

'Keep to the hedgerows,' Zis had said, 'then even if they're directly overhead they may miss us. Not too fast, a steady trot, and then you won't grow too tired.'

But Lark *was* tired, dreadfully tired, and very very frightened. It would be so terrible to get this far and be caught now. If only the sun would hurry, if only it would scorch down.

In fact the mist had begun to lift. A golden shimmer stole across the fields drenching grass and trees, cows were climbing to their feet and 'Listen,' Zis said,

91

'everything is waking.' A duck-egg sky broke above their heads, and birds struck up softly in the copses, tentative, practising, until the air was shot through with notes clear, silver, certain.

'How many daybreaks, how many dawns,' Zis said as he jogged comfortably, 'I have watched with my little master, steal over the Acropolis!'

'The — Acropolis?' panted Lark.

'A group of temples that crowns Athens — white, beautiful. Alexander was crippled, and his brother often carried him to the steps of the Parthenon, for that was his favourite temple. And we would lie all night beneath a wolf-rug, the boy and I, watching Artemis rising with all her train of stars.'

'You never told me how Ermyntrude caught you. Could you now, as we run?'

'Very good training for an athlete,' Zis grinned sideways at her, trying to hide his anxiety. Things were almost ominously quiet.

'Lark, I am old! Praxiteles, greatest of all Greek sculptors made me in the year of the 108th Olympiads; and though by tradition the prize was an olive wreath taken from a sacred tree in the precinct, he determined to gift me to the best athlete of that year's Games. It was there, on that rostrum in Olympia as I watched the youths compete, that I first knew that longing for life I think I shall die with...and there that I first saw Alexander.

'His family had brought him there from Athens, and every day Theo, his brother carried him to a seat on the arena's edge. Ah, how the child's eyes shone for the athletes! how narrowly he watched the flexing of a muscle, the wait before a leap; how he dreamed of flying through the air with the discus, the javelin, running with the fleetest runner!

'Five days the Games lasted; and on the fifth, when all the competitions — horse-race, chariot-race, sprints, long-jumps, boxing, wrestling, discus and javelin throwing — were done and won, the wreath was to be given. From my place on the rostrum I watched Alexander, pale and sad now, for it would be four long years ere the Games came again. The winner was a bold, dark-haired young man from Thessaly, and as the crowds cheered and, adorned with his wreath he received me, I felt myself *willing* him to notice the little boy, willing — I know not what.

'And he did; his gaze fell upon the child who could not walk or run, and on some god-given impulse he ran across the arena, thrust me into the little boy's hands. "Take him and place him above thy hearth; vow thou wilt grow as strong and finely-limbed as he!"

'Ah, Lark, that moment; never shall I forget Alexander's eyes.

'We returned to Athens, and day after day he exercised — days when his body ached, tears ran, he could no longer stand — and in the evenings Theo bore him to the Parthenon, to lie all night watching columns and sky, listening to silence, smelling the earth grow around us...and day would break again, rinsing the city, rinsing pain, and the sky over Athens would fill with swallows. — Look, there's one now!' Lark looked up to see not one, but three or four navy tails skim over the hedge above them.

'Bearing the dust of my city upon their backs,' Zis

said. 'Perhaps. Little by little Alexander grew well, his feet tough, his legs strong, his back as straight as a marble column. He began scouring the hills around Athens, outleaping the goats, and laughed, built a boat to pit himself against the whims of the moons and tides, boxed and wrestled with his friends: there was nothing he would not dare.

'When the Games came again, we journeyed once more to Elis; into Theo's safe-keeping he gave me, and when his young brother won his race, Theo leapt the balustrade and forgot me. And how, in his moment of glory, should Alexander remember?

'Evening fell, the crowds left. I was full of joy for Alexander's triumph, full of that sadness too, that Masha spoke of...and over the sea of olives Ermyntrude rode at last, into the empty Stadium like some dark avenging goddess. Nymph, I trembled, seeing in those seconds centuries of tyranny to come!'

'Oh why, why, *why* didn't Alexander remember you?' Lark was struggling against tears. 'And Katya, she forgot Masha...and Sarah, she — well, she did remember, but it was too late.'

'Children change, it's growing. They outgrow us,' Zis said gently.

'You must — love your land very much,' she was exhausted. 'I don't think I can go much further. What — what d'you hope to find, when you go back?'

'Sea! Sea round the islands,' said Zis. 'Freedom... columns to the sky. And smells. Nymph, look,' she followed his pointing finger, 'the sun!'

Blood-red it came, edging its way up over the far-away hills.

94

10

Lark's knees had buckled, she lay splayed on the grass in a hollow, like a handful of sticks someone had dropped.

'She'll have you, Lark, you and the Lifestone; you'll be dead as before. Come,' Zis urged, 'I'll carry you.'

'I'll fight her...I could fight her in about ten minutes, if I just had a little rest now. We could...fight her... together, Zis.' Her head flopped, she gave a tiny snore.

'Ancient Rhea!' But he doubted he'd get very far carrying her. 'Zeus be praised for that mist, they'll have had to keep to the ground to pick up our scent,' he thought. 'But when they start flying... If I could ambush them now before they take off, I could — I

95

will, I'll break the goose's wing.'

Wings…he remembered hours spent in the little skiff with Alexander watching the flight of seagulls, and up in the hills following kestrels and partridges, eagles and doves. He remembered with terrible homesickness the swallows over Athens.

But Ermyntrude must be stopped. He flung a handful of leaves over Lark, and doubled back the way they'd come.

Ermyntrude had lost Skite. They'd been following a country road.

'It's the only one,' Skite had said grumpily, 'and we'll have to go on foot till the fog lifts.' For a long time as he ran, beak to the ground sniffing the hedgerows, she'd grunted along behind, missing her old green broomstick, (which would no more have balked at fog than walked) lamenting the Lifestone, and cursing all wooden dolls, particularly French ones reared in Battersea. Then for good measure she'd cursed mists and geese, after which a swirl as thick as soup enveloped her, and when it disappeared Skite had too.

The sun had come swinging up over the hills: there was no time to howl, nothing to do but rush onwards, following her nose past sleeping cottages and waking farmyards, and then at last, away in a field of young corn she saw a white blob standing, gobbling as if his life depended on it.

Grass, he was at the grass again! With a yell loud enough to wake all the dead witches of Rezay, she shoved herself through the hedge, swooped down across the field and boxed its ears. The goose rounded on her with a hiss of outrage, butted her over in the corn, and chased her fourteen times round the cornfield.

Ermyntrude sat down on a large treetrunk, shaking.

How could she ever have mistaken that common, vulgar creature for Skite, her darling Skite, her winsome, web-footed wonder? Images of Skite, plump, handsome, white as snow as he'd been on the first day she'd found him, floated into her mind...then two or three strange things happened.

First there was a horribly uncomfortable, horribly *painful* pain in her chest, a sort of knot she could neither swallow nor cough up, in fact which wouldn't be moved at all; then her eyes began to sting quite dreadfully so she couldn't see, and lastly her nose started running. Big drips splashed down onto her socks, and when she put up her hand to wipe her nose she found her cheeks were wet.

'Badgers and broomsticks, the dew's still falling! *Plenty* of time. But if only I could find my dear little goose. Ah Skite, dear Skite, my little webbed wonder, where are you?' She had sudden, fearful visions of Skite being caught in a rabbit's snare, chewed by a fox, hit by a thunderbolt, or keeling over with a heart-attack, inches from Lark and the Lifestone.

But what good was the Lifestone, what good was *life,* without Skite?

'Skite, Skite,' her voice was a shadow of itself, 'Skite, where are you? It's Ermyntrude, your loving Ermyntrude come to save you!'

'Skite!' cried Lark at the very same moment. She sat up among the leaves.

'Lark!' said Skite; they stared at each other, blinking in the sunshine, for he had fallen over her in the hazel-tree hollow.

'Wh — what's happened, where's Zis?'

'Zis?'

'A bronze boy. He's helping me escape.'

'Did you run down the staircase with him?'

'He's helping me escape,' she said again, and then, 'Hallo. It's nice to see you, Skite. Even though I know you are on Ermyntrude's side.'

'I'm not really. At least — that is —' he felt a rat. 'I'm supposed to get the Lifestone from you,' he said miserably.

'I know, but I won't let you,' she jumped up and

brushed off the leaves.

'I'll have to fight you then,' Skite said even more miserably.

'Oh, must you? Oh dear. All right then — but you've got a beak and two wings. You'll have to let me get a stick, it's only fair.'

'I'll help you choose one.' They selected a nice swishy one from the bottom of one of the hazel trees, and Skite chewed it through with his beak.

'This looks a good flat place,' said Lark. 'Now then.' They looked at each other. 'Don't we have to step back ten paces?'

'Your size or mine?'

'We'll each do our own.' They both marched backwards from the middle of the flat place counting, then turned and faced each other. Lark began to feel rather nervous: she did a press-up, for she remembered Tom saying they built up your strength. 'Now then,' she said again.

'Just a minute.' The goose was preparing. He began to flap his wings, slowly at first, up and down, up and down, then faster and faster, standing on one foot and then hopping on it, little hops that grew higher and higher: and then he started turning, round and round hopping and flapping, higher and higher, faster and faster, and when he'd done three complete turns, he opened his beak and an extraordinary cawing sound came out — long, low, lamenting noises, which gradually grew into a concert of cackles becoming shriller and shriller, more and more excited, the wilder his hops and turns grew.

Lark watched open-mouthed.

'Just — puff — getting my blood up — puff,' Skite

explained between hops, turns, and cackles. 'I'm exhausted — and that lament was for whoever, puff, falls on the field — almost ready now — ready, yes, *charge!*' He rushed straight at a small tree stump which yielded not an inch, but the force of his rush hurled him backwards and he was down.

Lark helped him up; he was extremely dizzy.

'I don't think I'll bother with the blood-rousing bit this time. We'll just charge — ready, steady, —'

'No, I've lost my stick, wait!' shouted Lark. 'All right, ready, steady —'

'But *I'm* not ready,' said Skite. He really felt very peculiar. He sat down. 'You know,' he said, 'I think you're supposed to have a referee, or seconds, or something.'

'Let's wait then,' Lark said thankfully, 'till one comes along. Or two.' She sat down beside him, and then sprang up as though she'd been electrocuted. 'Skite, Skite, the grass — it's nearly dry!'

'What! Oh my beak and tail,' the goose sprang up too, 'oh, oh, oh, Ermyntrude will kill me, we'd better fight again!'

'But she can't do anything to you. I'll protect you, Skite. You're not really frightened, are you?'

'No, no,' said Skite, jittering. 'No, no, not a bit. No, I shall simply retire when all this is over — simply fly away.'

'Oo,' Lark said, 'you wouldn't be going anywhere near —' and just at that moment Zis tore into the hollow. 'Zis!' she cried, running to him joyfully.

'Lark, he gave her a hug. 'And the goose! — does he threaten you?'

100

Without waiting for an answer, the bronze boy grabbed the stick and ran at the goose. Skite gave a squeal of terror and backed up the bank, cannoning straight into Ermyntrude who, two fields away had heard his blood-rousing cackles, and come flying to the rescue.

'Skite, my treasure! Who dare threaten my white webbed wonder?' She flung herself in front of him and found herself face to face with Zis. 'The Greek boy!' she gasped. 'The hard one to torture,' for muscles are hard to pinch and how do you pull a bronze boy's hair?

Zis held his ground. 'You stopped my ears and nose with earth, and filled my eyes so I could not smell nor see.'

'So I did, so I did. Good, Greek, good! But now,' and she drew herself up reminding him of the Ermyntrude of old, 'touch a feather of this goose's head and I'll drop you into the hottest smelting furnace in Barrow-in-Furness!'

'Ermyntrude,' Skite stamped his foot. 'You're interfering. The wooden doll and I were just about to fight, and I'm forgetting what about.'

'Skite, my jewel, I'll fight the wooden doll for you.'

'But I don't *want* you to! You're interfering, go *away*, Ermyntrude.' He gave her a poke in the stomach with his beak, and then to his horror, for it had really been a very little poke, the old witch gasped and clutched her heart as though she had been mortally wounded (which indeed she had). She gave one piercing, terrible cry 'Wounded unto death!', and fell to the ground.

The toys and Skite froze.

11

Pain was quite new to Ermyntrude, and the one in her chest was worse than she could ever have imagined.

'I shall die of it, die of it,' she howled. 'Skite, Skite, you have stabbed me. Ah, I am stabbed, I am wounded unto death!'

Skite was stunned; proud, and at the same time terribly alarmed. 'It was only a poke, I only poked you Ermyntrude,' he mumbled over and over.

'I don't think I'll fight you after all,' said Lark edging towards Zis, but the bronze boy stood still as a stone, all his attention on the witch.

She was shaking so violently that the ground under their feet shook too, and all the hazel-trees quivered. Tiny, piteous moans escaped her, punctuated by sudden earth-tearing cries, deep sea-bed roars. Before their eyes she seemed to shrivel, grow suddenly wizened, and she covered her face as she sank to the grass. It was like watching a huge mountain split, and fall.

Then Zis ran across the grass, and gently prised her hands away.

'Ermyntrude!' It was a cry of wonder, and of triumph, softly he ran a finger over the folds of withered cheek. 'Ermyntrude — you are crying.'

'Not. Dew. Dew's still falling,' the old witch gasped.

'Nay, the dew is gone. Ermyntrude, you love. For you cannot cry, unless you love!'

'I'm not, I tell you,' she spat out between sobs. 'I'm a witch. I can't.'

'Then witch, thou art mortal... For Ermyntrude, you are crying.'

It was true, her tears fell in rivers. 'A goose, a goose, my witch-hood for a goose! Skite, my duck, my pigeon, live with me in a nunnery, I'll polish your beak and go on a diet, and you shall have rides on my shoulder.'

'But Ermyntrude, a nu — nunnery wouldn't suit me,' Skite stammered. 'I'm going to l — l — live in a farmyard.'

'Ah, to love in a pigsty! We'll *both* live in a farmyard. To be mortal, to be mortal, and love!' Tears streamed down her face as she stumbled towards him. Quailing, Skite scooted along the bank.

He gazed wildly about him but Zis had climbed a hazel-tree, and Lark was rooted to the spot; he tried to speak and nothing happened, he cleared his throat and choked. But when at last it came, his own voice astonished him with its strength and purpose.

103

'But I don't love *you*, Ermyntrude. I can't come,' he said.

There was silence in the hollow...then Zis began to hum very softly, the sad, archaic little tune he'd whistled in the attic.

The old witch had blanched dreadfully, Lark could not bear to look at her. There was a pain in her own chest, and she had never felt more aware of her own woodenness, not in her deadest days. Only her fingers crossed and recrossed over the Lifestone, as she wished for the goose to change his mind and hoped he wouldn't.

Then Skite said it again, very low. 'I can't come,' and Ermyntrude raised her face to the sky and gave one last, terrible cry.

'To a nunnery, to a nunnery!' she gasped. Gathering the shreds of her cloak about her, she turned, and staggered blindly from the hollow.

The sun poured down now.

Lark could feel it burning through the leaves on to her back...she bent her legs stiffly and touched the grass. 'It's dry,' she said sadly, 'but it didn't really matter anyway.' Skite sat on the bank with his eyes closed, and Zis, high up now in the hazel-tree, stared out over the fields.

'Will she really go to a nunnery?' Nobody answered. '...Because if she did, the nuns might have some geese. She could raise goslings. Not that it would be the same.'

'No,' said Skite.

'No,' said Zis.

No, thought Lark. Lotte could never be the same as

Sarah. Life was so inconvenient.

Skite opened his eyes at last. He felt terrible, but at the same time he was aware of a wonderful new sense of freedom.

Yet not so new...dimly he seemed to recognise it. Yes, it was very much as he used to feel years back, hundreds of years ago, when amongst the other animals he used to wander about the farmyard, chatting here, flapping there, pecking exactly when and where he wanted, and minding his own business.

Free, he was free!

No more pinching, no more feathers pulled, no more scoldings or tortures, or back-breaking journeys and all the grass he wanted. No, he wasn't going to be sentimental about Ermyntrude, but one of these days when he'd settled down in his farmyard, he'd go round all the nunneries and pay her a flying visit.

He flapped down from the bank, feeling much better.

'What are you going to do now, Lark?' he asked.

She told him, her heart plunging once more at the thought of it. 'You said you were going to fly away, Skite...where to?'

'To Battersea, wooden doll, with you if you like.' He owed her his freedom, and his death too, one day; besides, he liked her.

'Oh Skite, really?'

'I'll fluff up my feathers and as soon as you're ready,' he disappeared behind a bush.

'Zis...' she climbed up the hazel-tree where he still sat, staring out over the horizon. 'Zis, Skite says he'll take me to Battersea. Will you come?'

'No, Lark.'

'But you might love it. Sarah loves old things, she's like Philippe. And Tom, too. Couldn't you — try it?'

'Nay, I shall find the land of my gods. And you, will you not come with *me*?' She stared at him, too surprised to speak; he grabbed her and swung her round to face him.

'Lark, you will lose your *life!* And you love life, you've wanted it from the day you were made, how can you throw it away? You have freedom now, and *choice* — you can live as you believe, speak what you feel, do anything, everything you want. There's so much to discover, and you'll never find it out if you go back.'

'But I want to see Sarah.'

'You want to be owned.'

'I want to be *with* her. I want to go home.'

'To be owned.' His voice sounded scornful, and

somehow sad. 'Being owned's not equal. Not equal like
you were with T'ang, and Arabella, and Masha, and me
— not even like you were with Ermyntrude and Skite.
Life is too precious, Lark. It will never come back.'

But she shook her head stubbornly; he shrugged,
looking angry and disappointed, and something else,
lonely perhaps.

'Go then, nymph. And the gods attend you. I'll set
you on the way.' He swung his legs over the branch, and
shinned down the tree lithe as a monkey; Lark followed
slowly, feeling lost and unsettled. Life just now seemed
to be full of partings.

Skite was waiting at the bottom of the tree. Before
Lark could object, Zis had swung her onto his back. She
looked forlornly down at the bronze boy, and held up
the Lifestone.

'What shall I do with this?'

'Give it back to the sea whence it came. It will wash
up on some beach — perhaps,' he smiled, 'into some
other wooden doll's lap.' His eyes were suddenly shining
with tears.

'Oh Zis, I wish you'd come!'

'And I wish *you* would. Never mind, go,' he tapped
Skite lightly on the wing, glad now that he hadn't
broken it. 'Fare well, fly well, witch's goose, Lark's
goose!' He took her hand but she didn't trust herself to
speak and Skite began to flap his wings slowly, then
more and more strongly.

'Hold on! Hold on, Lark,' he cried, and she held
on for dear life to the ruffle of feathers round his neck,
feeling that wonderful, frightening lurch in her stomach. He plummeted straight upwards through the

107

cluster of hazel-trees that formed the hollow.

'Goodbye, goodbye!' Zis was standing in the middle of the flat ground she and Skite had nearly fought on, eyes shielded against the sun as he waved.

'If you —'

'I can't hear!' she shouted, and he cupped his hands to his mouth: 'If you change your mind, look for me in the Parthenon at full moon!'

Then the bronze boy ran lightly to the spot he'd dropped the fighting stick, picked it up, and climbed the bank. A moment later he was out on the open road, and picking up speed, he began to run fast and surely towards Athens.

'Skite, I know this place!'

The goose was circling over a rambling, overgrown park...yes, there was the farm, and wasn't that Lotte swinging a couple of dolls on the farmyard gate? And there was Philippe running out of the cowshed, and he was carrying something in his hands with infinite care — T'ang, dear, wise T'ang!

And there were the slate roofs —

the chimneys —

the turret...

Lower and lower Skite flew, dipping, gliding, seeming to stand almost motionless in the air for moments on end, and the little château, the 'toy château', Lark's Castle glittered up towards doll and goose in the hot morning sunshine as they gazed and gazed...

Then Skite flapped his wings strongly once more, and they flew high over the elms, heading for the North and England.

108

EPILOGUE

Tap, tap, there it came again.

Sarah sat bolt upright in bed. Tap, tap, she craned her eyes through the dark, it was coming from the window, tap, tap, a bird trying to get in? What else could be out on a window sill five floors up in an Edwardian block of flats?

She grabbed her dressing-gown and stumbled over in the dark. Stupid! Why hadn't she put on the bedside light? Heart pounding, she drew aside the curtain.

Lark, her wooden doll Lark, whom she'd lost in the heart of France! And good heavens, there was a goose on her windowsill.

'Sarah, Sarah, it's me, it's Lark!' The wooden doll

was jumping up and down and thumping on the pane; frantically the little girl fumbled with the catch, pushed up the window, and doll and goose tumbled over the sill onto the floor.

'Lark, what — how — but you're cold! Come under the eiderdown (if you like),' she added politely to Skite who, to her astonishment said 'Thank you.'

'Sarah, this is Skite. You saw him flying over the chimney,' and as she warmed up under the bedclothes, Lark told her how she had come to life, and everything that had happened in Lark's Castle afterwards.

'Oh you are *lucky*, Lark what an *adventure*,' Sarah cried enviously. 'I've just been at school, and Tom's moved up a form, and Laura Brown's left, and I've missed you and it's been awful. Oh it's lovely to have you back, I'll never ever lose you in my life again, and no one will believe it when they hear you speak!'

'But I can't stay,' Lark heard herself say.

Skite who, though he thought it tactless of Sarah to have a goosefeather eiderdown, had dozed off, gave a squawk of astonishment and fell out of bed.

'Can't stay? Can't stay?' the little girl whispered. 'Lark, why?'

'I — I — oh dear, I don't know!' Lark had turned quite pale, she was as shocked and bewildered as the little girl.

'I only knew it this moment — but oh yes, I *do* know why. I want to *live*, Sarah, I can't bear to give up life now and the Lifestone won't work for me if I let myself be owned. You see, oh dear, I want to choose things and decide things for myself, I want to learn and discover and share, I want to move, and shout, and laugh and

110

cry and sing! And Zis was right, I love you, Sarah, more than anyone, but I can't go back to being a thing; I wouldn't be able to share things with you, you'll be growing, but I won't be because nothing will be happening to me and in the end, in the end,' Lark's eyes were full of tears, 'you won't treat me like a person because I won't be.'

Sarah sat very still under the eiderdown; she had tried so often to imagine what it was like being a doll and it was just like being her. Except she felt older than Lark, and much, much younger and she was determined not to cry.

'Sarah, I never dreamed this would happen.'

'It's all right, I think it's all right, I do understand. At least — oh bother!' and then she too, burst into tears.

'Dear, oh dear, oh dear,' Skite hopped up on to the bed again and patted at each of them awkwardly in turn. 'Oh my beak and tail, never mind never mind Sarah, I'll bring her back to see you.' He flopped gruffly over the window and busied himself fluffing up his feathers.

Still crying, the little girl carried Lark over to the sill. 'Where will you go, Lark?'

'I have a very important call to make,' said Skite at once. 'To a nunnery. Near Rezay.'

Lark sniffed, then laughed. 'Rezay first...' Full of love and sadness, she gazed at the little girl, but there was so much to say she couldn't say any of it, and anyway Sarah knew.

She climbed on to Skite's back.

'Don't say goodbye, just ready, steady, go!' Skite cried and took off.

Lark's tears flew out behind her like a train of little stars but she was laughing too, as she turned and waved. She would come back one day she knew it, but she'd come back *live,* as she'd go away again live, and she knew Sarah would have chosen to do the same.

'Give my love to Ermyntrude and Lark's Castle, and Zis!' the little girl cried, and leaning out of the window as far as she could in her cotton pyjamas, she watched goose and doll grow smaller and smaller as they wove their way away from her between the dark shapes of a London night.

And at last they were only a tiny white blob disappearing behind one of the chimneys of the Battersea Power Station...

Pocket inside
last page.